Gregory Mcdonald

FLYNN

Gregory Mcdonald is the author of twenty-five books, including nine Fletch novels and three Flynn mysteries. He has twice won the Mystery Writers of America's prestigious Edgar Allan Poe Award for Best Mystery Novel, and was the first author to win for both a novel and its sequel. He lives in Tennessee.

FLYNN

Gregory Mcdonald

VINTAGE CRIME/BLACK LIZARD

Vintage Books

A Division of Random House, Inc.

New York

FIRST VINTAGE CRIME/BLACK LIZARD EDITION,
FEBRUARY 2003

Copyright © 1977 by Gregory Mcdonald

Library of Congress Cataloging-in-Publication Data
Mcdonald, Gregory, 1937–
Flynn / by Gregory Mcdonald.
p. cm.
1. Flynn, Francis Xavier (Fictitious character)—Fiction.
2. Aircraft accidents—Investigation—Fiction.
3. Police—Massachusetts—Boston—Fiction.
4. Boston (Mass.)—Fiction. I. Title.
PS3563.A278 F5148 2003
813'.54—dc21
2002033143 *9920*

Vintage ISBN: 0-375-71357-3

Author photograph © Nancy Crampton

www.vintagebooks.com

Printed in the United States of America
10 9 8 7 6 5 4 3 2 1

To Chris and Doug

One

"Good night, Grover. I'm sure you're right."

Flynn slammed the door of the black Ford.

"It must be nice to be an experienced policeman." Muttering, he went through the gate, along the walk, and up the steps to the porch of the large, dark Victorian house which loomed above him. "Even of low rank."

The Ford accelerated noisily up the two-o'clock-in-the-morning street, and screeched around the corner to the left.

"You'd think somebody wanted him home," Flynn said to himself.

While he was working the key in the lock of his front door, a jet airplane taking off from Boston's Logan Airport across the harbor thundered only five hundred meters above his chimney.

"Oh, God," Flynn said. "I want my tea."

However long he lived there, Flynn heard the noise. Some people, some of his neighbors, were able to put it out of their consciousness as a driver after a while no longer sees the windshield wipers. Others, more painfully conscious than their neighbors, would have a new round of protest meetings every few weeks.

Flynn neither failed to hear the airplanes nor did he attend protest meetings.

He just suffered.

In the living room, lit only by the light from the hall, he gazed at his cello, leaning against the curve of the baby grand piano.

Once, at two o'clock in the morning, when they first moved here, he had spent a half-hour playing his cello. Neighbors complained—even some who had long since stopped hearing the airplanes. Their message, firmly delivered to Elsbeth the next morning, was something on the order of, "Not jet airplanes and the cello, too— not at two o'clock in the morning!"

"Ach, well," said Flynn. "Where's my tea?"

The kettle itself was keeping him company, still burbling and hissing on the range, when he was half-way through his cup, although he'd turned the knob. Elsbeth had left out the fixings.

Another jet shrieked overhead.

Who would want to leave Boston at two-thirty in the morning?

Of all the cities he had left, he did not remember ever taking off at such an ungodly hour.

"Da?"

Jenny was in the door.

The blue saucer eyes now sleepy, the golden curly hair now tousled, the skin of her cheeks a little creased from her pillow, Jenny, at twelve going on thirteen, had missed the awkward phases all her life, with perfect skin and perfect, growing teeth, a perfect little body, and was about to miss the awkwardness of being thirteen, from all appearances: proper, of course, as Jenny would be, even at this peculiar hour in her own kitchen, a bathrobe pulled almost around her, an undone package, a present carried under her arm.

"It's yourself, is it?"

Sleepily, she climbed into his lap.

8

"I had a present."

"A present? Now who'd send my bag of fluff a present?"

She pulled the plain white card from the mess of paper and cardboard under her arm.

"It says, 'I. M. Fletcher.' That's a funny name."

"Fletcher, is it? That is a funny name."

"When you speak to I. M. Fletcher, are you supposed to call him U. R. Fletcher?"

"I see you've been studying your French declensions."

Only Jenny could make him laugh at quarter to three in the morning, especially after Flynn had just arrested a perfectly nice man who had kindly murdered his sick old mother, even laying her out on her own bed, gray hair flowing on the pillow, before calling the police on himself.

(Grover had been right, of course: The man should be charged with first-degree murder. Mercy murder was not to be recognized, ever; there were too many who would take advantage of it. Flynn had argued for a charge of murder-with-love, whatever that might mean to a court. Flynn knew precious little about the workings of courts.)

"The last time I saw your man Fletcher, he was calling himself Peter."

"Do I know him?" Jenny asked, no part of her mind concerned with the problems of a nice man who had kindly murdered his sick old mother.

"He came here on a Sunday. The day we did the Beethoven F major. You may remember, Eighteen—One."

"Oh, he was nice. All tight and golden."

"Tight and golden?"

"Like a rubber band."

9

"Here, let's see what the card says."

Using the back of her wrist, as if she were well used to favors delivered at the door, she passed him the card.

"Let's see, now. On the back, in handwriting, it says, 'Jenny, may I be the first to present you with something too expensive—Fletch.' My God, what could it be?"

Jenny sat up enough to rummage around in what was appearing more every moment to be wastepaper.

"Mother says it's very expensive."

She pulled forth from the tissues a ruby and diamond pin.

She held it out to her father in the palm of her hand.

"My God. Let me look at it."

Flynn held it to his eyes.

"My God. I think it's real."

"It came from Rio de Janeiro. I'm not sure where that is."

"It's in Brazil."

"Well, it's very nice of him."

"It is that."

"I wanted to show it to you."

"Can you afford the insurance?"

"Why did he send me such a thing?"

"Well, Jenny, I'll tell you. Mister Fletcher is the marrying kind."

"Is he?"

"Ah, yes. He's been known to marry one or two."

"And will he marry me?"

"It rather seems he means to try."

"It's very nice of him to send me a pin so soon."

"You can't wear it."

"Mother said the same thing."

"Well she should."

"But, Da, there's a school play."

"I'm sure there is."

"I'm to play the princess. And Ms. Berger said to bring a lovely jewel from home to adorn me if possible."

"No such thing is possible. Nothing could adorn you, Jenny."

"But it's a lovely jewel, like she said."

"Your mother's costume stuff can adorn you enough."

"But I rather like this pin, Da."

"So would all the rest of the world's beauties, my darling, but few ever see such a thing, let alone possess it, and never at the age of twelve-and-a-half. Here, I'll keep it for you."

He put it into his jacket pocket.

"Mayn't I have it? Even for the play?"

"You may have it when you're twenty-one."

"Not even eighteen?"

"Only if there's a need to pay your tuition. Now, what are you doing up, other than being robbed of your jewels?"

"I wanted to show you."

A long white form appeared in the kitchen door. It was yawning.

"Da?"

"Oh, my God. Another one. And the kettle's off."

"My violin was stolen."

"Come in."

The boy moved into the light, lanky and blond at fifteen, hair sticking up, rubbing one eye with the base of his fist, barefooted, and, being without Jenny's sense of haute costume, pajamaed without a robe.

Even without seeing them, Flynn could tell his twin sons apart from the difference in their voices. Randy's was a mite slower than his brother's. His violin playing was a mite more precise than his brother's, but not much. Other people had to rely solely upon Randy's hair being a mite blonder, not much, his nose a centimeter longer.

He sat in the opposite kitchen chair, his elbows quickly finding the table, the area above his jaws, forward of his ears, finding the heels of his hands.

"What do you mean, your violin was stolen?"

"From my locker. At school."

"At Cartwright School?"

"Yes."

The other voice, Todd's, sounded in the door.

"It's true, Da."

The twins always defended themselves, each other, however it worked, even when neither challenged nor attacked. Flynn had taught them that. Crawling around the floor with them as babies, he had taught them to outflank any aggressor to either or both.

"Things have been missing for weeks now," Todd said.

Flynn looked at three of his five children, fully aware it was three o'clock in the morning. Precious gems and violins were all very well, but there were other matters and their mother to face in the morning.

Randy said, "It was a good violin."

"It is," said Flynn.

"Wasn't it insured?" asked Todd, arms folded under a yawning mouth in the kitchen doorway. Always the flanking action.

"It was not," said Flynn. "And why wasn't the locker locked?"

"It was," said Randy.

"All the lockers were locked," flanked Todd. "In all the robberies."

"There have been many robberies?"

"Dozens in the last weeks, Da."

Looking into the bottom of his teacup, for once

Flynn wasn't sure which boy had spoken.

It didn't matter.

They were together.

"What's missing, besides Randy's violin?"

"Money. The money Juan's father sent him from Mexico." Apparently, Todd was beginning a great list.

"Was that much?" asked Flynn.

"Three hundred dollars."

"That's immoral!" announced Flynn, not hesitating to protect himself against further assaults.

"It's for the whole term."

"I've never spent three hundred dollars loosely in my whole life."

"You're not Juan," yawned Randy.

"Mark's soccer ball, Jack's plane ticket home to London, Nicker's pot stash, Ted's—"

"What?"

"His stash of pot," interpreted Randy.

"It was a lot of pot, Da. Over two hundred dollars' worth," said Todd.

Yawning bored, the boy who had his violin stolen put propriety to youthful, illegal possession. "His Dad sends him to school with it. They grow it on their place in Virginia."

"And do you use it?" asked Flynn.

"Only sometimes," said Todd. "On math review days."

"My God, why did I come home?"

Randy, who was always one for sticking to a point, said, "My violin was stolen."

He wiped his nose with his left hand. He should have been taught piano, thought Flynn, by his mother.

It's the devil's own job to steal a piano.

"Indeed," said Flynn, "you children have entirely too many possessions."

13

"Not us," said Randy, suddenly awake. "I had my violin, and it was stolen." And he looked pathetically angry. "And it was a good violin."

"It is that," said Flynn, with satisfaction.

Todd said, "You should find it, Da."

"I? Why I?"

"We," amended Randy. "Like before."

Flynn picked up his cup to drain the dregs of his camomile.

"Cartwright's a private school," he said. Jenny was getting softer in his lap, as neither a ruby and diamond pin nor talk about a stolen violin was capable of keeping her awake beyond three in the morning. "What goes on there is private. The Boston Police has no right to interfere there unless called in. I think."

The teacup smashed in his hand.

Jenny's body tightened against his chest.

The kitchen table moved closer to his vest.

Randy's face fell forward from his hands.

A flash of light appeared through Elsbeth's curtains, in the window over the sink.

There was a painful explosion.

There was blood coming from the base of Flynn's hand.

In the doorway, Todd screamed.

Immediately, they were standing in the window of the dark dining room.

The moonlight was reflected on the surface of the harbor.

In the sky above the harbor a mass of yellow flame was whipping up from a huge, hot-red and silver falling bulk.

For the moment, Flynn was one with his children, young, in Munich, seeing unrooted flame hating itself, escaping itself, leaping up from itself.

14

Small objects, pieces of freight, people, some of them originally on fire, had blown away, downward from the plane, and were falling down the sky, extinguishing themselves. They sprinkled the moonlit surface of the water.

Despite the thousands of times he had heard the sound, he remembered specifically he had heard this particular plane taking off.

"A plane has exploded," he said to his children. No matter how old he got, there would be new things he couldn't handle, old things he had never been able to handle. "It's all right," he said stupidly at the window with his children. "A plane has exploded."

He picked up Jenny.

The children had to know what they were seeing.

Burning, dying people were falling into the harbor from the sky.

"It's all right, boys," he said.

The flaming, thrashing object that had seemed suspended in the sky so, becoming larger, darker as it came closer, hit the water in three pieces, setting up six separate walls of spray in the moonlight.

Steam rose from only one section—the biggest.

In the light, Flynn saw Todd's eyes huge.

Holding Jenny, he tried to put a hand out to each of his sons. And found he could. Jenny was clutching to his neck on her own.

Under his hands, both boys were shivering.

It was only then he heard Elsbeth upstairs, screaming in her bed, in Yiddish, *what to do, what to do,* some prayers, in Hebrew, reacting to a war in the Middle East she had survived, which had finished.

"It's all right, Elsbeth!" he shouted insanely in German. "It's just a plane crash!"

He heard the baby, Jeff, cry.

15

Two

"What's in the shoe box, Da?"

It was on the dining room table, next to his coffee cup. He had not dared leave it anywhere else.

"The trouble with having a father as ideal as I am," Flynn said, whacking his boiled egg with his knife, "one who tries to answer your every question with the fullness of perfect honesty, is that on that rare, if not unique occasion when I absolutely cannot answer you, I discover I am without even the normal paternal abilities to lie, dissemble, or evade."

"Yeah," Todd said, "but what's in the shoe box?"

"The only response I can think of at the moment is the considerably rude line: none of your business."

Randy said, "You're not going to tell us what's in the shoe box?"

"I am not."

On the other side of his plate was the morning edition of the Boston *Star*. There was no mention of the airplane explosion. It had happened too late to make the final edition.

Seeing the facts of the accident reported baldly in black and white this morning might calm them all down.

Both Randy and Todd were white and pinched-faced at their places at table, not eating much.

Jenny was still looking as if she wanted to give herself into a lovely cry. She had several times already and had been told by her mother enough was enough.

Winny, at age nine, was mostly disturbed by having slept through the whole thing.

"You are to be commended," his father had said. "It does little for one to see an accident one can do nothing about."

At first light, Flynn had gone through his kitchen door into the backyard.

Except for Winny and the baby, Jeff, none of them had slept. It remained too early for breakfast, an interminable time.

He had sat with his children enough.

He had seen about fixing the window in the kitchen.

Even then, small boats were clustered on the surface of the harbor—Police Harbor Patrol, the Fire Department, the Coast Guard—moving back and forth, grabbing what evidence of the accident they could. The explosion had happened in midair; most of the evidence had sunk below the surface of the water.

Near his seawall Flynn found a hand.

It was lying on the cement skirt of the seawall, palm up, neatly severed at the wrist. Three or four dots of blood were on the cement where the wrist should have been. Obviously, the impact of the hand landing on the cement had squirted these few remaining bits of blood from their casing.

Drained, white—nevertheless, the hand seen all by itself, soft, puffy, apparently undamaged, seemed bigger than real.

It would appear to be the right hand of a middle-aged man, Caucasian, probably a business executive or a member of one of the professions. The palm was soft, devoid of callouses. The fingernails had been manicured professionally.

There was no ring.

Muttering, "You should pull yourself together, Charlie," Flynn carefully went over the rest of his yard, the rocky beach, and examined the roof of his house to be sure there were no other bits and pieces of humanity around to shock his children.

It had been difficult, interrupting Elsbeth while she was getting breakfast, getting her attention, asking her where she kept small boxes, like a shoe box, without telling her why he needed it.

Elsbeth entered the dining room with a plate of toast and more orange juice.

"No one's eating," she said.

Flynn said, "I'm eating."

"Your life is full of corpses, Da," said Randy, staring at his plate. "You're up to your hips in them all the time."

"Not all the time," said Flynn. "I'm apt to step aside when I'm eating."

At her head of the table, Elsbeth smoothed her apron over her thighs. "Enough is enough," she said.

"Already," Flynn said.

"It happened." As she spoke, she looked at each of the children. "A very terrible thing. A great tragedy. Especially a big shock for those of you who had the bad luck to see it. And since when are so many people who should be in bed asleep awake and in the kitchen at three o'clock in the morning? These parties when your father comes home I didn't know about. You should have been in bed, asleep. Then you would not have so much hurt this morning. You were up, you saw it: your bad luck. There was nothing you could do about it then; there is nothing you can do about it now. If a plane had exploded last night in India or Ohio instead of over your house, maybe you'd hear about it on the news, say, 'A great tragedy, Receive them, O Lord,' and never think about it again. That's what you're to do here. Forget it. This terrible accident has nothing to do with you. You should be concerned with matters more at hand."

"Amen," Flynn said.

"Now, eat," she said.

The children moved closer to the table. Todd took a piece of toast.

Despite her speech, Elsbeth continued to sit back from the table a moment, looking at her empty plate.

"Speaking of matters closer at hand," Flynn said, wincing, "we don't seem to have a spare piece of glass for the kitchen window in either the basement or the garage."

"I'll get a piece of glass," said Elsbeth. "The kitchen is cold. We're heating the outdoors."

"The point," said Flynn, "is that I expect the local supply of window glass will be exhausted by ten o'-clock. If the explosion broke one of our windows, it doubtlessly broke hundreds of other windows."

"I know how to stand on line," said Elsbeth.

Flynn said, "You're not taking your own advice."

"I know. I'm sorry. It takes a moment for wisdom to sink in. Especially when you make it up yourself."

"You're not eating," Jenny said.

"I nibbled in the kitchen."

Randy passed her the plate of toast and she took a piece.

"While you were out in the yard, the Commissioner called, Frannie."

"He's up early."

"He said he's at the office already. He wants to see

19

you immediately. Sergeant Whelan also called. He heard from the Commissioner, too. He's on his way over to pick you up. He should be here."

"The Commissioner," said Flynn, "can eat applesauce."

"You have something better to do," asked Elsbeth, "other than keep your job?"

"I thought I'd tell Grover to drive me over to the boys' school."

"Cartwright School? When the Commissioner calls before seven in the morning saying he wants you?"

"I want to make sure the Case of Randy's Violin is being looked into."

"The Mysterious Disappearance," said Todd.

Winny said, "The Violin Case."

"It's a terrible thing, stealing a violin," said Elsbeth. "It's almost like stealing a person. Who would do such a thing?"

"That," said Flynn, "is what I mean to find out."

"You said last night the Boston Police couldn't do anything about it unless the school asked," Todd said.

"I mean to interview your headmaster," Flynn said. "What's-his-name, Doctor—?"

"Jack," said Todd.

"Jack?"

"Jack Lubell."

"You call your headmaster 'Jack'?"

"Some of the kids call him 'Ding-Dong-the-Bell.' "

" 'Ding,' for short," added Randy.

"Or 'Dong,' " amended Todd.

Flynn said, "In a private school, where I pay tuition on top of taxes, you call your headmaster 'Jack'?"

"Or 'Ding-Dong,' " said Jenny.

"This is a democracy, Da," said Randy. "Everybody's equal."

20

"If your headmaster's your equal, then why is he your headmaster?"

"Pilpul," said Elsbeth.

"No," said Winny. "Pupil."

"You go to a private school, dressed in blue jeans and sneakers like shoeshine boys—"

"They have nice sweaters," said Elsbeth.

"You're fifteen years old, you don't know how to tie a necktie, you couldn't spell your way out of a flower garden, and you call your headmaster 'Jack'!"

"Or 'Ding-Dong-the-Bell,' " said Jenny.

"Everyone dresses this way," said Todd. "And Jack tells us to call him 'Jack.' "

"Furthermore," said Randy, "they're not called 'Headmasters' in this country, Da. They're called 'Principals.' Spelled p-a-l. Your principal is your pal."

"Oof," said Flynn. "If he's my pal, then why does he keep sending me tuition bills?"

"Speaking of your natural sense of aristocracy," Elsbeth said, "the man who starches your shirts has gone out of business. Second one this year."

"There's no respect," said Flynn.

"You just told the Police Commissioner to go eat applesauce," said Jenny.

"That's another thing," Flynn said to Elsbeth. "Did you see what that indecent man sent Jenny?"

"Yes. The pin."

"Sending a thing like that to a twelve-and-a-half-year-old girl."

"It's beautiful," said Elsbeth. "Priceless."

"It's indecent!"

"Mister I. M. Fletcher was very nice to send me such a nice pin," said Jenny, carefully picking a scab off her elbow. "I intend to marry him."

Flynn heard the front door open and close.

"What? Marry that rubber band?"

Sergeant Whelan came through the door from the front hall.

"And what," said Flynn, "are you doing in my dining room at eight o'clock in the morning?"

"Good morning, Inspector."

"Good morning, Grover."

"The Commissioner wants to see you immediately."

" 'The Commissioner,' is it? Shouldn't we call him 'Eddy'?"

"You can, if you like, sir."

"Would you like some coffee, Sergeant?" Elsbeth asked.

"Thank you, Mrs. Flynn, but we haven't time."

"Indeed, we haven't," said Flynn, standing up with his shoe box. "We're driving the boys to school, on the way."

"But, Inspector—"

"Grover, I have had quite enough debate since I entered this house six hours ago, and not one wink of sleep. I'll have no debate from you."

"My name's not Grover."

Flynn handed him the shoe box.

"Here, let me give you a hand."

Three

"Come in, Frank."

Police Commissioner Edward D'Esopo stood up behind his desk and held out his large hand.

"Good of you to come as quickly as you could."

It was ten minutes past nine.

"I was obliged to drop the kids off at school," Flynn said. "It took only a moment."

He put the shoe box on the Commissioner's desk and shook hands.

The Commissioner was almost as big as Flynn, bull-chested, with lively brown eyes under brown curly hair that dripped onto his forehead. However, his midsection suffered from too many hours behind the desk, and too many long dinners in behalf of department public relations.

"Would you like some coffee?"

"I've had my cup, thank you."

"You know Captain Reagan, of course."

Reagan, a man near retirement, sat in the full costume of a Captain of Police in a side chair. He could either lead a parade or be laid out, altering nothing but his posture.

"Morning, Frank."

Flynn sat in the hard leather chair facing the desk.

"I suppose you know what you're here for?" The Commissioner's question appeared rhetorical.

"Rotation," answered Flynn.

"What's rotation?" the Commissioner asked the Captain.

"Never heard of it."

"Whatever you'd call it," Flynn continued to answer. "Getting that benighted son of childless parents, Grover, out from under me and providing me with an assistant who has at least mastered the alphabet in English."

"Grover?" the Commissioner asked the Captain.

"Sergeant Whelan," Reagan answered. "Now, look, Frank. Sergeant Whelan is a competent policeman, a basic nuts-and-bolts cop who did well at the Academy. He was born and brought up here. You come from somewhere outside the city—Washington, was it? Chicago?—and even though the record of arrests and convictions you've had while you've been with us has been astounding, we all know, despite the uniqueness of your rank—arranged for you by the Commissioner himself, here—and your independent little office over in the Old Records Building, that you haven't had that much actual police training or experience, you don't know the city—"

"Is Grover also the nephew of Captain Walsh?"

"He's a good cop, Frank," Reagan said. "A while with you will make him a terrifically valuable man to the Force—"

The Commissioner glanced at his watch.

"I don't want to talk about this. Frank, what were you going to do this morning?"

"Take a nap."

"What?"

"I got home at two-thirty. The airplane explosion had us up all night—"

"That's right. You live in Winthrop, don't you? How's Elizabeth?"

"Fine."

"The kids?"

"Fine."

"It's the airplane explosion I wanted to talk to you about. Do you have anything, any other cases you can't put aside?"

"Just a matter of theft," Flynn answered. "A violin."

"What?" Captain Reagan said. He jumped forward in his chair.

"I was up late last night sitting shiva with a poor wee man who mercifully had suffocated his ancient, dying, pain-wracked mother with a pillow."

The Commissioner looked at him sideways.

"It doesn't sound like a major case."

The Captain slapped his knee and laughed. "And tell me, did 'Reluctant Flynn' have the heart to arrest the bugger?"

"I left it to Grover," answered Flynn. "He derives a satisfaction from muscling the momentarily errant."

"Christ." The Commissioner rubbed his temples with the heels of his hands. "When what's-his-name learns the alphabet to your satisfaction, I'm going to have to ask him to teach it to me. I have no idea what you just said."

"His name is Sergeant Richard T. Whelan," Flynn said. "Due for promotion. Out from under me."

"Frank." The Commissioner's tone of voice was of one who had abandoned rhetorical questions forever. "A Zephyr airliner blew up last night over Boston Harbor. It had just taken off from Logan Airport."

25

"At ten minutes past three this morning, to be more precise," Flynn said.

"What else do you know about it?" the Commissioner asked.

"I saw it. I heard the noise and looked. I am, therefore, at least a partial witness."

"Good," said the Commissioner.

"Not at all good," said Flynn. "What else is known about it?"

"Not much else. It was a flight to London. A passenger flight. A 707. That right, Captain?"

The Captain blinked his red-rimmed eyes.

Commissioner D'Esopo said, "We threw everything out in the harbor first thing, Harbor Patrol, fire boats. The Coast Guard was there immediately, although I understand there wasn't a chance of survivors. Already this morning I've arranged for professional divers to be flown up from an oil rig off Nantucket. In fact, they should be out there working by now. I've told them to bring up everything they can find."

"God." Captain Reagan rubbed his eyes. "Horrible thought."

"They might find some old cases of tea," smiled Flynn, "on which His Majesty's tax has not yet been paid."

"The Navy is sending a full crew of divers up from Florida. They should be here later today."

"The Navy is very excited," said Reagan.

"Shit," said the Police Commissioner. "Some damned wire service reported this morning the possibility the airplane was shot down."

"Shot down?" said Flynn.

"By a rocket," laughed Captain Reagan. "Fired from a submarine."

"Some old boy out too late in Dorchester says he

26

saw a red streak come up from the surface of the water just beyond the harbor mouth and hit the airplane," the Commissioner said. "Why the hell the press feels it has to print everything every half-assed inebriate says—"

"The Navy's got submarine chasers strung out from Newport, Rhode Island, to Bath, Maine." Captain Reagan's red eyes were wet with mirth. "They're having a high old time. Ah, well," he said. "Any excuse for a serious drink ashore. I was in the Navy once myself."

"Somehow," Flynn said, putting a match to his pipe, "this doesn't sound a matter for the Boston Police."

"It isn't," concurred the Commissioner. "The possibilities are too many and too big. To this point we had to be Johnny-on-the-spot."

"Then what could you possibly want from me?" asked Flynn, lowering his soft voice to the nearly inaudible.

The Commissioner said, "We don't want to end up on the spot, if you get me. The Federal Bureau of Investigation is sending in a team this morning. So is the Civil Aeronautics Board. They're on their way now, all on the same airplane."

"Sure, it's imprudent to put that many important people on the same aircraft."

Frank Flynn and Eddy D'Esopo grinned at each other.

"Frank, you've had experience with the federal types before."

"I know you think so," Flynn said.

"Well, whatever it was you were doing before you became ours, you have more experience with the federal types than us poor slobs who worked our way up from the beat. You speak their language."

"You mean, they speak German with a lilt?" asked Flynn.

"I think they do," said Reagan, stretching out his legs. "I think they do."

"You want me to be a baby-sitter," said Flynn.

"I want you to be liaison for the Boston Police Department." The Commissioner looked at his watch again. "The first wave of feds is arriving at Logan Airport at ten-twenty. I said you'd meet the plane."

"I see."

"Zephyr Airways has arranged for a hangar so the bits and pieces taken out of the harbor can be laid out for examination. The hangar is already under tight security."

"Although nothin's in it," said Reagan.

"Zephyr has also arranged a conference room at the airport for use of the investigators. That also will be under tight security. The Airways' liaison man's name—" the Commissioner referred to a piece of paper on his desk—"is Baumberg. Nathan Baumberg."

"Is Nathan Baumberg a public relations man?" asked Flynn.

"No. He's a vice-president of the airlines in charge of airplane maintenance or something. An engineer. On the phone this morning he sounded young and badly shaken."

"Good," said Flynn.

"I've asked the Massachusetts Port Authority to take care of the press. They've been given a room fairly far away from both the hangar and the conference room. As yet, they don't know where the hangar is."

"You're obstructing the public's right to know," said Flynn.

"I'm just protecting our right to find out first," said the Commissioner. "You'd better be off."

28

"I'm off."

Flynn stood up and headed for the door.

"It's time I had an easy assignment like this."

"Captain Reagan will make sure you're not bothered by any other cases while this is going on."

Rising from behind his desk, the Commissioner picked up the shoe box.

"Frank. You forgot your shoes."

From the door, Flynn said, "That's not my shoes."

"Your lunch, then."

The Commissioner opened the shoe box.

His mouth and his eyes opened wide, simultaneously.

He dropped the box.

It landed on an edge and the human hand flopped onto his blotter.

"Christ!"

"Who'd have such a thing for lunch?" Flynn ambled back across the large room. "A little something I found this morning in my backyard."

He replaced the hand in the box, and tucked the box under his arm.

Crossing to the door again, he said, "Grover should have had it at the lab by now. I remember giving it to him once."

Four

"Airport," Flynn growled.

"Oh, no."

Behind the wheel of the black Ford, alarm replaced the usual expression of general distaste on Grover's face.

"Oh, yes."

Flynn settled in his seat.

"The Commissioner didn't assign the air crash to you, did he?"

"It was a midair explosion, not an air crash," said Flynn. "And he did."

Grover's face worked only when it was taut with anger, yelling at someone, usually as close to the other person's nose as possible. Normally, it looked like an eaten half-grapefruit in a kitchen sink.

"He wouldn't do that."

"He did."

"Oh, no."

Flynn said, "I think maybe it's time you started the car."

By fighting his way into the speed lane, Grover put them into the thickest traffic and immediately had to stop.

Flynn said, "We're meeting a gaggle of FBI's. By the way, do you call them 'Fibbies'?"

"No," said Grover, staring at the license plate of the car stopped in front of them. "We don't."

"You should," said Flynn. " 'Fibbies' and 'Cabs.' "

" 'Cabs'?"

"Civil Aeronautics Board."

"Oh." Grover blew the horn. "We don't call them that, either."

"I thought you wouldn't."

"What's the first thing we should do on a case like this, Inspector? Where do you think we start?"

"Well, now, I was hoping you'd ask. The first thing I want you to do is get me a map of Boston."

"Yes, sir."

"Then I want you to put a red dot on the map for every pawnshop in the north and what they call the east sides of the city."

"Pawnshop?"

"I want you to locate every pawnshop precisely on the map. And I want you to draw a blue circle around each red dot representing every pawnshop nearest a bus stop or a subway station. Have you got that?"

"What have pawnshops got to do with an air crash?"

"You'll see."

The car went forward a length.

"What time are we supposed to be there?" Grover asked. "I mean, at the airport."

"Twenty minutes past ten."

Grover looked at his watch.

"Good God!" He flicked on the siren and jounced the car over the curb onto the road divider. "It's ten-fifteen."

"I thought you'd do that," said Flynn.

"What?"

The car slammed off the divider and darted through the red light at the intersection.

"Turn it off!" shouted Flynn.

"What?"

"Turn the damned thing off. That's an order!"

Grover turned off the siren. The car slowed to a more sedate pace.

"The noise," said Flynn, "is painful to my ears as well as to my sense of dignity. It is neither my purpose nor my intention to allow myself to be dragged through the city in a vehicle screaming like a cat with its fur afire!"

"You've said all that before," said Grover.

"Have I, indeed?"

"You have."

"Then it's time my sentiments regarding the siren were seared on your soul! You flick the damned thing on every time your blood pressure approaches vitality. Watch that truck!"

They swerved.

Grover said, "I wouldn't have to 'watch that truck' if the siren was on!"

"I know," said Flynn. "He'd have to watch out for you, and him I don't trust at all."

Grover's face was tightening. He banged the steering wheel with his palm.

"I was thinking about you while I was waiting for you while you was with the Commissioner," he blurted.

" 'Was' you, indeed?"

"How come you got so much money?"

"Have I got much money?"

"You live in that big house in Winthrop. You've got five kids. You send them all to private schools—"

"Not Jeff. He's only ten months into life."

"I've heard Todd, or Randy, whichever of them it was—"

"Commonly referred to as 'Todd-Randy Which-

32

ever,' " said Flynn. "Officially, in the school records, as 'The Flynn Twin.' "

"—mention you have a farm in Ireland, for Christ's sake—"

The car swooshed down the ramp into the long tunnel to the airport.

Flynn waited until they came up the other side.

"Some detective you are," he then said. "Working foot-in-mouth with me all these months and you haven't yet discovered I'm corrupt."

Grover held out his badge to the man in the "Official Cars Only" toll booth.

"Another thing." Grover rolled up his window as vigorously near slamming it as he could. Even Grover couldn't give the full impression of slamming a car window up. "Why are you an Inspector, and why are we stuck over on Craigie Lane, in the Old Records Building? Why aren't we in a Precinct, or over at Headquarters with the other guys?"

"That's two questions," said Flynn. "Both of which have the same answer."

The car radio buzzed.

Flynn took the microphone off the hook.

"Good morning," he said into it.

"Eddy D'Esopo, Frank," said the Commissioner's voice.

"I've already said 'Good Morning' to you," said Flynn.

"Frank, it's on the radio that one of the passengers aboard that plane last night was Judge Charles Fleming."

"Oh?"

"He was a federal judge, Frank."

"That's just below the Supreme Court, isn't it?"

"An important man, Frank."

33

"A political appointee?"

"Yup. A presidential appointee. Another celebrity aboard was Daryl Conover."

"The actor."

"Yes. Currently playing *Hamlet* at the Colonial Theater. Or was. What he was doing on a plane to London at three o'clock in the morning is unknown."

"Hamlet made a decision, alas. Sweet Will never meant him to."

"That's all, Frank. You'll be hearing more from either me or Reagan."

"Cheerio."

Flynn replaced the microphone on its hook.

"That's no way to speak to the Commissioner," Grover said. " 'Cheerio.' Jesus."

The road between them and the ZEPHYR AIRWAYS sign was clogged with television vans, press cars, the cars of the curious, and of furious, legitimate travelers —all held at bay by police cars.

"I spoke to the Commissioner about you, Grover."

Draped over the wheel in the stopped car, Grover said nothing.

"I asked that you be considered for promotion."

Slowly, Grover turned his head and looked at Flynn full-face. "You did?"

"I did. Do you think I'd pass up an opportunity like that?"

Flynn fumbled around under the dashboard.

"Why don't you turn on the damned siren?" he said. "You think we can sit here all day?"

Five

The conference room at Zephyr Airways was over-heated and overlit. Despite the sunlight streaming through the thick floor-to-ceiling, wall-to-wall window overlooking the runways, the room was filled again by fluorescent lighting that ran around the ceiling next to the walls, plus five more fixtures across the center of the ceiling. Both ceiling and walls were off-white, relieved only by framed cardboard reproductions of airplane photographs. Each plane had ZEPHYR AIRWAYS painted on its side.

The room was dominated by a huge, elliptical, polished wood conference table—almost a landing field in itself.

At one shoulder of the table was a visual-aid easel. There was an illustration of a 707 on it.

More than a dozen men were standing, lounging in the room, most with jackets off and ties askew, drinking coffee from cardboard cups. They ranged in age from twenty-five to forty-five; all had the same builds, slim with weight lifters' chests and shoulders; the same haircuts, just long enough to be parted with calipers; the same muscle-jawed faces which could have been achieved only by the continuous belaboring of chewing gum.

These, then, were the Fibbies and Cabs.

The most insolent-looking man sat on the conference table, one foot on a chair, near the door, surrounded by somewhat younger coffee drinkers.

"Flynn," Flynn said to him.

"Local police?"

"Yes."

The man snorted in disgust at the table. "You could have gotten here on time. What have you been doing, out buying yourself a pair of shoes?"

Flynn tried to hand the man his shoe box.

Instead, the man's eyes engaged his with a furious stare.

"Look, Flynn, all we want from you local jerks is a little basic cooperation. Ground support. When you're supposed to meet a plane at ten-twenty, you meet a plane at ten-twenty!"

A single glance told Flynn that Grover was turning pale. It was the kind of chewing-out the Sergeant always believed effective.

"Let me lay down a few ground rules," the man continued. "First, you'll be available to us at all times. Second, you will stay out of our way, confining yourself to doing what you are told to do, when you are told to do it. Third, you will see that the Boston Police Department provides all services we ask, the minute we ask for them. Fourth, you'll keep the other jerk members of the Boston Police in line. We don't want any locals bucking for heroes' stars on this case. Fifth, you'll keep the press, both local and national, as far away from us as possible, and then some, at all times. Is that clear?"

Flynn smiled. "And tell me, did your father indicate to your mother what his name might be the night he spent with her?"

The men stared at Flynn. Some stepped back.

36

An older man, still wearing his suit jacket with his tie tight, stepped from the glare of the room into the group.

"Inspector Flynn?" He put out his hand. "Jack Rondell, FBI." While shaking hands, he asked the man whose legitimacy Flynn had questioned, "Have you briefed the Inspector, Hess?"

"Yes, sir."

"Good, I'm sure you'll be a great help to us, Inspector. Boston Police has a wonderful reputation. Everybody's here. Let's get the briefing underway."

Flynn handed the shoe box to Rondell, who delegated it to Hess, who delegated it to the man standing beside him, who passed it to the man behind him, who passed it to the man beside him, the youngest of all, who opened it, looked inside, turned pale, swayed, fought to refocus his eyes a moment, and fainted.

"Poor Ransay," said Rondell. "First field assignment, isn't it?"

After Ransay had been taken out with the evidence and the rest of the men had settled themselves around the table, Nathan Baumberg introduced himself as a vice-president of Zephyr Airways, in charge of maintenance, and the man next to him as Paul Kirkman, who had been in charge of passenger services during the time the London flight had been loading.

Kirkman was a trim man, surprisingly well shaved, considering he had been on duty since midnight, and wearing a shirt which appeared fresh.

Baumberg, standing at one shoulder of the table, his back to the light from the window, had a razor nick on his left cheek, earnest, troubled eyes, a shirt button missing over his paunch, and sleeves that appeared to have been rolled up and down several times.

"First," he said, "let me tell you what we have, and then Paul and I are here to field any questions you have."

"This isn't a press conference," said Hess.

"Do you have any better way of doing it?" Baumberg asked.

"Let's have a little cooperation," Hess said.

"Go on, Mister Baumberg," Rondell said.

"Yes, sir."

"Zephyr Flight 80 to London passenger loaded at two-forty A.M., eastern standard time, for a three-ten A.M. departure."

Q.: "How many passengers were aboard?"

Kirkman: "The plane was full. That means forty-eight first-class passengers, sixty-two coach passengers, and a crew of eight."

Q.: "There were one hundred and eighteen people aboard?"

Kirkman: "Yes, sir."

Q. [Flynn]: "I take it from the radio that you've already made up a passenger list?"

Kirkman: "No, sir. It's being duplicated now. We'll have copies for you in a few minutes."

Q. [Flynn]: "Names plus addresses?"

Kirkman: "Yes, sir. Addresses as well as we have them. People aren't always too cooperative when they put down their addresses. Well, I mean, for tax purposes, if they're traveling on business they're apt to put down their business addresses."

Q. [Flynn]: "Why would anybody want to fly to London at three-ten in the morning?"

Q. [Hess]: "Shit!"

38

Kirkman: "You mean, why was there a flight at three o'clock in the morning?"

Q. [Flynn]: "Precisely."

Kirkman: "This particular flight has three feeder flights connecting with it, one from Atlanta, one from Chicago, and one directly from San Francisco."

Q. [Flynn]: "Then only a small percentage of the passengers originated their flight in Boston. Do you have any idea what that percentage might be?"

Kirkman: "Not yet, sir. A check of the addresses on the passenger list should tell you."

Q. [Hess]: "Let's get on with the questioning."

Baumberg: "The forward and central cargo holds had been loaded by the four-to-midnight shift. Therefore, they were closed and locked by midnight. The stern cargo holds were not closed until three A.M., just before takeoff. They were used for the passengers' luggage."

Q.: "What was the cargo?"

Baumberg: "We don't know, specifically, yet. Manifests are being gone through. A list will be prepared."

Q.: "Was there any dangerous cargo aboard?"

Baumberg: "No, sir. Absolutely not."

Q. [Hess]: "If you don't know what the cargo was, then how do you know there was no dangerous cargo aboard?"

Baumberg: "Against company policy. Dangerous cargo is never put aboard a passenger flight."

Q. [Hess]: "Bullshit."

Baumberg: "The four-to-midnight maintenance crew were responsible for this aircraft. Their maintenance reports were filed before midnight, and had been checked by my assistant by twelve-forty-five. There was absolutely nothing unusual about them. Everything checked perfectly. The midnight-to-eight crew went over the

39

plane again between two A.M. and three A.M. Again, everything checked out perfectly."

Q.: "What time did they file their reports?"

Baumberg: "Just after the plane blew up."

Q.: "Mister Baumberg, were airport security devices in perfect operation last night?"

Kirkman: "Yes, sir. I watched the loading myself. There was nothing unusual or suspicious. Some of the passengers, especially from San Francisco, were a bit jolly—"

Q.: "What does that mean?"

Kirkman: "Well, they had already been in the air some hours, and had had their drinks—"

Q.: "Was the luggage scanned?"

Baumberg: "Yes and no."

Kirkman: "The carry-on luggage was scanned. Nothing suspicious there."

Baumberg: "Systems for scanning the luggage we put in the cargo holds are not very good. We usually scan only boxes or suitcases that, for some reason, cause suspicion."

Q.: "Did any of the cargo luggage cause suspicion this morning?"

Baumberg: "Not that we know of. Of course, most of the luggage for this flight came straight from the feeder flights. The passengers didn't get near the luggage between flights. There would be no reason for suspicion."

Q.: "In fact, the passengers' luggage, which was to go into the cargo holds, wasn't scanned at all?"

Baumberg: "We may have to tell you that, after we check."

Q.: "So, Mister Baumberg, do we understand that this airplane had had no flight previous to this flight, Flight 80 to London?"

Baumberg: "Yes, sir, I mean, no. This aircraft had just flown from London, arriving Boston at five-forty P.M."

Q.: "Were the same crew to fly it back to London?"

Baumberg: "No, sir. It was an entirely fresh crew. The crew that arrived from London yesterday afternoon will take tomorrow morning's flight back."

Kirkman: "If there are any passengers."

Q.: "When was the plane last serviced?"

Baumberg: "You mean, a complete overhaul?"

Q.: "Yes."

Baumberg: "Six weeks ago. Complete overhaul. Everything checked: engines, wiring, frame, skin—"

Q.: "Did they find anything unusual?"

Baumberg: "No. I went over the reports this morning. The plane was in A-1 shape."

Q.: "Mister Baumberg, is there any idea yet how this explosion happened?"

Baumberg: "No, sir. There are divers now going over the impact site. The Navy is sending a planeload of divers and equipment up this afternoon. I mean, they're arriving early this afternoon. The Coast Guard is moving a dredge-platform onto the site. Zephyr Airways has donated Hangar D for your use—"

Q.: "Nice of them."

Baumberg: "Anything found relating to the explosion will be brought there for your inspection."

Q.: "I don't suppose the aircraft's flight recorder has been found yet?"

Baumberg: "No, sir. And I'm not sure how much use it will be to us when we do find it. The plane was in the air for less than a minute."

Q.: "And it wouldn't have taken off unless all systems were 'Go'?"

Baumberg: "Of course not. I did listen to the con-

41

trol tower's tape of Flight 80 this morning. Absolutely nothing unusual about it."

Q.: "What did it sound like?"

Baumberg: "Absolutely routine."

Q.: "Was there no pilot reaction? I mean, to the explosion?"

Baumberg: "An intake of air."

Q.: "You mean, he gasped?"

Baumberg: "I guess you could say that. The pilot gasped. Copies of the tape are being made."

Jack Rondell, one hand over the other on the table, said, "Well—"

"Ah—" Baumberg seemed hesitant to speak. "A newspaper reported in a late edition this morning that an eyewitness, in Dorchester, saw a rocket hit the plane from just outside the harbor."

"Sure," Hess said. "Sure, sure, sure, sure. You were shot down by BOAC."

A girl had entered the room and was giving each of the men a copy of the passenger list.

"Well," said Rondell. "I guess the first thing we had better do is make complete reports to our directors."

"Grover, step along to the people who sell flight insurance and get the names and amounts of anyone who bought insurance for himself on Flight 80 last night. Now isn't that what an experienced policeman would do?"

"Yes, sir."

They were standing in the Grand Concourse of Zephyr Airways, each holding a passenger list.

42

"I'll take the car and return to the office. You get yourself back however you can."

"Inspector, I don't think you should have called an FBI man a bastard."

"And why not?" Flynn lit his pipe. "He called you a jerk."

Grover said, "It's not often a local policeman gets a chance to work with the FBI on a big case like this."

"I don't expect I have much of a future with the FBI."

"But maybe I do have."

"Ach, now there's an idea. Yes, indeed. Maybe you do at that."

Flynn was looking toward the door of the conference room.

"Here comes the bastard now."

Hess was walking with a man on each side of him, one step behind him. "Flynn!"

Flynn had begun to walk toward the main door of the Concourse.

"Where are you going?"

"I am going," said Flynn, "to try to solve one hundred and eighteen murders."

Six

Cocky had left a note on Flynn's desk: "CALL CAPT, REAGAN."

"Ah, la."

Flynn glanced across his huge, ancient, paneled office at the cot in the alcove next to the fireplace before switching on his desk light.

"Woe is me."

As he dialed Police Central and waited to be put through to Captain Reagan, he swiveled his chair to look through arched windows at the harbor.

Tugboats were pushing a work platform out to the impact site.

"You wanted me?"

"Hi, Frank. How did the meeting go?"

"The Fibbies and Cabs are getting busy right away on complete reports to their directors."

"Good, good." The Captain hadn't really heard him. "Thought we should let you know. The HSL is issuing a statement taking credit for blowing up that airliner last night."

"And what the HSL is that?"

"Ah, I think it means the Human Surplus League. One of these crazy groups in Cambridge. Out to save the world by destroying half of it."

"Did you say Human *Surplus* League?"

"Yeah. They keep announcing there are too many people in the world. Their motto is 'People Are The Problem,' it says here. Guess they mean to do us in by the planeload, Frank."

"There are too many people in the world, is that it?"

"Something like that."

"Well, they might be right at that. The question always is: Where do you start?"

"Seems they started last night with Zephyr Flight 80 to London. I don't pretend to understand these kooks, Frank."

"Is it a big group, do you think?"

"Intelligence says it has to be. Posters have been appearing all over Boston and Cambridge for weeks now. Circulars have been stuffed in mailboxes. A huge campaign."

"And how does such a group take credit for such a thing? Do they call a press conference, rent a hotel ballroom, and serve wine and cheese?"

"Someone called the Boston *Star* an hour ago from the HSL and said a statement taking credit for the explosion had been left in locker 43 at the bus station. One of the editors and a couple of our boys are there now."

"And I suppose the HSL or whatever it is will be given publicity for this whether they blew up the plane or not."

"Of course. The *Star*'s holding an edition."

"What more is known about the Human Surplus League?"

"Not much. Nothing."

"Can't their posters be traced? Through a printer or something?"

"Everything's homemade. They use cardboard from boxes, paint from spray guns you can get anywhere.

Their circulars are usually typed on a Selectric and duplicated on a number of different machines. I have one of their circulars here."

"What does it say?"

" 'Do The World A Favor—Drop Dead.' "

"Advice they might consider taking themselves, under the circumstances."

"Well, we haven't cracked them. As I say, they're new to the area. Only been here about six weeks. We're checking with other police departments to see if anyone has any experience with these people. All we can say is they appear to be one of these mass-murder cults. It would explain the senseless killing of over a hundred people, Frank."

"Yes. It was dramatic enough."

"I'll call you when I get a copy of their statement, Frank. Read it to you."

"That's all right," said Flynn. "I can buy the *Star*."

Cocky entered, dragging his left leg behind him, carrying a cup of tea in his right hand.

"Ah, Cocky," said Flynn. "An answer to a prayer."

Cocky spilled a little of the tea on the folded towel Flynn had on the edge of the desk for just that purpose—for Cocky to spill on it.

"That's lovely," said Flynn.

Detective Lieutenant Walter Concannon, while arresting counterfeiter Simon Lipton (actually while reading him his rights in the living room of his home), had been shot in the spine by the counterfeiter's nine-year-old son, Petey.

Lipton was sent to prison, Petey to a home, and Detective Lieutenant Walter Concannon was retired, his left side partially paralyzed.

Flynn had never met the man, but he stopped by the

46

retirement celebration for Cocky one night on his way home, and had a few quiet words with him about chess.

The next morning at nine, Cocky limped into Flynn's office on the third floor of the Old Records Building on Craigie Lane, a hand-tooled, wooden chessboard and chess set under his right arm.

While Flynn said nothing, but watched, Cocky set the game up on an unused table at the side of the office.

A half-hour later he returned with two cups of fennel tea on a small tray in his right hand.

He set a cup on each side of the chessboard.

Then he moved Pawn to King Four.

Cocky had been in the office ever since, answering the phone, taking messages, making tea, typing the occasional letter with the fingers of his right hand, always impeccably dressed in one of his old patrolman's suits, white shirt, and tie. He was a wizard at research.

Flynn suspected Cocky had set up a room for himself somewhere in the building, a cot, a chest of drawers, a hot plate, but he never asked. Times he had invited Cocky to his home, for a Sunday musicale and dinner, Cocky had always refused.

And the chess games had continued. Sometimes Flynn won.

Flynn took his tea.

"I see you finally moved your Bishop," he said.

The right side of Cocky's face smiled.

Without picking it up from the desk, he was scanning the passenger list of Zephyr Flight 80.

"Murder isn't enough," said Flynn. "Now it has to be mass murder. Simple murder doesn't make the headlines anymore."

"Percy Leeper." Cocky pointed to a name on the list.

"Now who might that be?"

Cocky opened the morning newspaper he had left on Flynn's desk to the sports section.

Flynn had never known whether Cocky was taciturn as a result of being shot, or if he had always been short of words. He was a great one for showing rather than telling.

The main headlines were: LIMEY COPS WORLD MIDDLEWEIGHT CROWN—*Leeper TKO's Henry in Ninth.*

Center page was a large photograph of a boxing scene. Knees and arms straight, one man was falling back, heading for the canvas.

The other man, in stance to hit again, had a perfect boxer's body, with light hair splayed over his ears and a marvelously mashed nose.

"So that's Percy Leeper," said Flynn. "World Champion at midnight, a charred corpse falling through the sky three and a quarter hours later. A theme worthy of Chaucer, Cocky, but somehow I don't find it comic."

Flynn looked up the telephone number of the Cartwright School.

"A federal judge, a Shakespearean actor, a world champion athlete. 'Surplus humans'—I don't believe!"

A woman, doubtlessly an office secretary, answered the phone.

"Cartwright School. Good morning."

"Good morning. This is Mister Flynn. I need to speak to either of my sons, Randy or Todd."

"I'm sorry, Mister Flynn. They can't be disturbed. They're in the play yard."

"What did you say?"

"I said, they can't be disturbed. They're in the play yard. This is their soccer period."

"I heard what you said. My asking you to repeat

was solely a device to see if you'd have the bald-faced courage to do so. Now that I see you have, allow me to repeat myself. I said I need to speak to one of my sons. I did not phrase it as a matter of whimsy. I did not say, if one of my sons happens to be standing next to you with an ear cocked I might put a word in that ear. I did not say, if one of my sons happens not to be engaged at the moment I would like to speak to him, as I presume the school to which I send my sons keeps them engaged in one pursuit or another more or less continuously. I did not say, if it is convenient for you I would like to speak to one of my sons, as what is convenient for you at the moment is of little relevance. Lastly, of most importance, I did not ask your permission to speak to one of my sons, as I do not now and never will need the permission of you or anyone else to speak to one of my sons. Now, if I have made myself sufficiently clear, get one of my sons to the telephone in the quickest manner of which you are capable."

There was a digestive pause.

"One moment, Mister Flynn."

Cocky was grinning.

Hand over the mouthpiece, Flynn said, "I'm a bully, right? I get bloody sick of every mother's child answering the simplest request with an insubstantial 'No.' It's an automatic response. Go up to anyone on the street and say, 'Say "yes" or "no",' ninety-nine out of a hundred of them will say 'No.' "

"If you actually did that," Cocky said, "you'd be arrested."

"Would I, indeed?"

"It's called Open Solicitation."

"I hadn't thought of that. Well, there's entirely too much law, too."

"Da?"

Todd was panting.

"Are you both on the soccer field?"

"Yes."

"Good. All sweaty and smelly?"

"Yes."

"Grand. I don't want you to shower. Either of you."

"Why?"

"I thought you might ask that. Because I want you to do a job for me."

"Great."

"I want you to go home directly after school, maintaining your present odor of soccer, get dirty jeans and whatnot out of the laundry hamper, put them on, put the rest of them in knapsacks, and get onto the subway."

"Okay."

"At precisely five o'clock this afternoon, I want you to come up out of the subway in Harvard Square. Grover will be there, inadvertently, of course, radiating the fact that he is a flatfoot of the meanest disposition. He will yell at you, pursue you, and proceed to arrest you. I want you to make as much of a scene as possible. Run in opposite directions, yell, let him catch one of you. Rough him up. You won't mind doing that, will you?"

"No."

"Now's your chance. I don't know why I always give the best jobs to other people."

"Is he to arrest us?"

"No. You're both to escape. Separately. Then stay separate."

"What are we doing?"

"I'm sending you underground. I want you to find a charming group of people supposedly doing business in

50

Cambridge calling themselves the HSL—the Human Surplus League."

"There was something about them in the newspaper the other day."

"There's something about them in the newspaper today, too. They're claiming credit for blowing up that airplane last night. Charming group."

"If either of us finds the group, are we to penetrate it?"

"Yes. You're on the lam from the fuzz, you see."

"I've got it."

"If one of these kindly underground citizens' groups doesn't pick you up within the hour, begin inquiring of the street people where you can crash for the night. Is that the right word—'crash'?"

"Right on."

"Thank you. If you make enough of a scene with Grover, you should be picked up fairly quickly. If not, I expect the story of your escaping the fuzz will have enough currency, quickly enough, to gain you entrée in even the most undesirable home."

"Then we follow our noses to the HSL?"

"Yes. The headlines in today's paper, particularly the Boston *Star,* will give you a reason for bringing the topic up. Express admiration for them."

" 'Cool,' " Todd said. " 'I dig that scene. I gotta get with them, Man.' "

"Words to some such effect. Do your best. Be careful. Call your mother every day at four o'clock."

"Yes, sir."

"Remember: don't take a shower."

Cocky was still studying the passenger list.

"Find anything else interesting?" Flynn asked.

The phone rang.

Flynn said, "Hello?"

"Thirteen?"

"Yes."

"N. N. here. One moment."

It was less than a second's wait.

"Frank?"

It was N. N. Zero.

"Yes, sir."

"Can you meet me at Hanscom Airfield?"

"Yes, sir."

"I should be there in an hour."

It was twelve-thirty-five.

"I'll be there."

Flynn hung up.

Hand still on the receiver, Flynn said, "Huh!"

Cocky said, "Anything wrong?"

"Yes," said Flynn. "My teacup is empty."

Cocky glanced quickly at Flynn, and left the room, with the teacup.

"Elsbeth?"

"I got the window glass. I didn't even have to stand on line. Such a wonderful country. Plenty of everything for everybody."

"N. N."

"Oh?"

"Zero."

Without pausing, she said, "Shall I pack a bag for you?"

"I don't think so. I'm meeting him in an hour. Wanted you to know."

"In case you disappear."

"Also, I've asked Randy and Todd to do a job for me."

"Oh?"

"Something called the Human Surplus League is taking credit for the air explosion last night. I asked the boys to go find out who and where they are. It might take a few days."

"Oh, Frannie. Is it necessary to use them?"

"Elsbeth, these people may have murdered one hundred and eighteen people."

"I suppose so. Will they be safe?"

"Sure," Flynn said. "These people are only interested in mass murder."

Seven

Grover entered the office carrying a brown paper bag.

"Where's Hanscom Airfield?" Flynn asked.

"Out Route 2."

"How long will it take us to get there?"

"Half hour. Less. I brought sandwiches for us."

"And did you bring one for Detective Lieutenant Walter Concannon, Retired, Sergeant?"

"I forgot. I got chicken salad for you."

He was taking sandwiches wrapped in paper out of the bag.

"But that isn't the big news," Grover said. "Guess who boarded that airplane last night after trying to take out half a million dollars' worth of flight insurance?"

"The pilot?"

"No."

Grover bit into his roast beef sandwich.

"That means I have only one hundred and seventeen more guesses, right?"

Cocky entered with the cup of tea.

"The Honorable Charles Fleming. Judge Fleming."

"You don't say! The Justice might not be so honorable?"

Cocky put the teacup on the towel.

"Grover brought you a sandwich, Cocky," Flynn said.

Cocky glanced at the sandwich on Flynn's desk and the half sandwich in Grover's mouth, and snorted.

Flynn said, "Then I'll eat it myself. What was the Honorable's address?"

Grover checked his notebook.

"The Meadows, Wood Lane, Kendall Green."

"Has a nice ring to it. Sylvan."

"Expensive."

"Where's Kendall Green?"

"Out Route 2."

"Near the airfield?"

"No."

"Did you say this is a chicken sandwich?"

"Chicken salad."

"Well, the chicken escaped with his life in the making of this sandwich. Very little indeed was taken off his hide. What are these green lumps in it?"

"Celery."

"That's the salad part, is it? All held together by a white paste it looks somebody has already masticated."

"That's mayonnaise, Inspector."

"The great thing about American prepared food is how completely it's prepared. It's even pre-chewed."

Grover said, "You don't like your sandwich?"

"Well, there are three of us famous detectives standing over it, and any one of us would be hard-pressed to discover the chicken in it."

"It cost a dollar and a half," said Grover.

"Your father should have taught you not to waste your money. Now, were there any other passengers aboard that plane this morning who had either the foreboding or the prescience to insure their last few breaths?"

"One." Grover checked his note pad again. "A guy named Raymond Geiger, lived in Newton, insured himself for five thousand dollars."

55

"Well," said Flynn, "five hundred thousand dollars to one man might equal five thousand dollars to another. Still, half a million dollars is a lot of money. You buy this sort of flight insurance through machines, don't you? Feed it quarters or something?"

"Dollar bills," Grover answered.

"Oh, yes, of course. The only thing you can get for a quarter these days is two dimes and a nickel."

"I expect other people were insured for that flight, Inspector."

"Oh, yes?"

"Remember that a percentage of the passengers, probably most of them, were through-passengers from San Francisco, Chicago, Atlanta."

"Yes. They would have taken out insurance for the whole flight wherever they started it. I'm afraid we'll have to leave much of that to the Fibbies. The things we can do on this case are strictly limited."

Grover said, "It really is a case for the FBI?"

Flynn said, "Yes."

"I mean, it is entirely in their hands?"

"Yes."

"Only they have the resources, Inspector, to solve it?"

"Yes."

"I mean, all we're supposed to do is help them out however we can—not go off on our own?"

Flynn said, "Yes."

Cocky was standing over the game of chess, studying it.

Flynn said, "You heard that the Middleweight Champion of the World, the English boxer, what's-his-name, Percy Leeper, was aboard that plane?"

"The FBI guys were talking about it after you left, Inspector. That was some fight last night."

"Did you see it?"

"I was with you last night, Inspector."

"Oh, yes. So you were. And the HSL, the Human Surplus League, has notified a newspaper that they were responsible for blowing up the plane this morning. The little darlings."

"Bunch a little cock-suckin', mother-fuckin' sons of bitches."

"Oh," said Flynn, "do you know them?"

"I know their type."

"They believe there are entirely too many of us on earth, and sometimes I'm not entirely sure they're wrong."

Grover said nothing.

"Entirely," said Flynn. "Which reminds me. This afternoon at five o'clock, I want you to meet Randy and Todd, who will be emerging from the subway in Harvard Square at precisely that moment, carrying knapsacks, and make a noisy attempt to apprehend them."

"Arrest them? You want me to arrest your sons?"

"No. I want you to try very hard to arrest them, creating as big a scene as you can, and fail."

"Inspector—"

"I'm sending the lads underground, Grover. In pursuit of the HSL."

"They're your kids, Inspector."

"They are that. Fine lads, too."

"Inspector, it is wrong of you to use your own kids on an investigation."

"You've mentioned that before."

"Wrong, wrong, wrong. Against Department regulations. There's no way to protect them."

"I'm sure you're right, Grover. But, you see, I've got a peculiar contention. I was striking a few blows

57

for righteousness when I was a lad, and I don't see why they can't have a few early whacks themselves. Life isn't all Brahms, you know, and any Da who raises his kids thinking so is doing them no favor."

"It's wrong, Inspector."

"Think of it as a family tradition," Flynn said. "And do what you're told, as a means of beginning a few family traditions of your own.

"In the meantime," Flynn continued, "I remind you that I want a map of Boston with a red dot indicating every pawnshop, especially in the north and east sides of the city. I want a blue circle around the red dot for every pawnshop particularly close to a public transportation system. Have you got that?"

"I don't see what it has to do with the explosion of the airplane."

"Ah," said Flynn. "The Lord and Police Inspectors work in mysterious ways. Now, after this magnificent repast you so thoughtfully provided of celery, goo, and air-blown bread, do you think we can find Hanscom Airfield?"

As he stood up, Flynn crumpled the goo-smeared sandwich papers into a ball and dropped it into the wastebasket.

Flynn said, "Do you see what my next move is, Cocky?"

Over the chess set, Cocky grinned at him.

"You're not telling me, is that it?" Flynn looked at the board. "I'll figure out something."

"Inspector," Grover asked, digging car keys out of his pocket, "why are we going to Hanscom Airfield?"

"To see an old friend of mine," Flynn answered, "who's dropping by, just for the moment."

Eight

RAMP TO RUNWAYS OFF LIMITS EXCEPT TO AIRPORT PERSONNEL.

"Go down there," Flynn said.

"It's off limits."

"We won't get run over."

"We haven't identified ourselves to airport personnel."

"I daresay they'll ask."

It was one-thirty-three.

Grover jerked the steering wheel and stepped on the accelerator. The car darted down the ramp.

"I expect that's the plane now."

"Inspector, that's an F-100. A fighter plane."

"Yes, you're right about that. I'm surprised you know."

"Who are you meeting?"

"Wait here a minute, and see where the plane ends up."

"It will come up here, of course, to the buildings. It has to report in."

"Let's see if it does."

The plane used little of the runway in landing, turned off at the first intersection, turned left again, and taxied downwind to the line of trees at the very edge of the field.

Heavy clouds were scuttling across the sky.

Grover was looking through his rearview mirror.

"Here come the Air Police."

"Go meet the plane," Flynn said.

"What about the AP's?"

"Ignore them for the moment. Mustn't keep the man waiting."

Grover drove the car at a furious speed down the main runway.

"While I'm talking to my friend, doubtlessly the Air Police will give you ample opportunity to explain. Be sure and apologize, Grover, for not checking with them first. Tell them you're always making mistakes."

"Not me, buddy."

The plane was still closed when they arrived at its side. The jet engines were whirring down.

Flynn stood on the runway.

The roof of the cockpit rose slowly.

N. N. Zero released himself from his seat belts and electronic headgear.

N. N. Zero had to have a working communication system wherever he was.

"Hello, Frank."

"Sir."

N. N. Zero was three feet, ten inches high.

He had his own method of getting down from the plane, as the footholds were too far apart for him. He would hang from one hand, find a foothold with one foot, use his hand on the next foothold, and hang again.

Flynn always had the instinct to help him, whatever he was doing, as he would a child, but had learned a long time ago that such was a most grievous insult.

Flynn had worked long and intimately with John Roy Priddy—N. N. Zero.

"I brought you some tea, Frank."

"Grand."

The little man took off his gloves and unzipped a pocket in his flight suit.

"Papaya Mint. Ever tried it?"

"I have, sir."

"Well, here's some more. Drink it in good health."

"Thank you, sir."

"How's Elsbeth?"

"Fine."

"Randy?"

"Fine."

"Todd?"

"Fine."

"Jenny?"

"Fine."

"Winny?"

"Fine."

"Jeff?"

"Fine."

"You look a little tired, Frank."

"I'm not. I'm just short of sleep."

"Ah, like the old days, eh, Frank? Before you and I got so high-ranked life became nearly impossible for us. Mawlaik, Khairpur, Mafeking, Suakin. Did we ever sleep, Frank?"

"Infrequently."

John Roy Priddy had no family.

And he hated sleep.

As over-thin as he was over-short, he would fight sleep for days and nights at a time. However long he had postponed sleep, however exhausted he was, he would dream terrifying dreams, sweat profusely in his sleep, groan, and scream heartrending screams. In his career, he had undergone three courses of physical torture, in three different countries, administered by three different sets of experts, each incident lasting a month or more.

And when he woke, John Roy Priddy always heaved himself dry, vomiting whatever or nothing, frequently just air, his stomach muscles working convulsively.

Flynn had watched his friend over many years, in many parts of the world. Priddy's way of life had never changed. And Flynn had never spoken of it.

Of course they never slept in the old days—which weren't that many months ago.

Priddy would never sleep, if he could help it.

"Raw wind," N. N. Zero said.

Flynn shrugged. "Boston."

An Air Police jeep was roaring down the runway toward them.

"Let's walk a little," Zero said.

"Aye."

They walked along the edge of the horizontal runway, the line of trees to their right.

"What do you know about the explosion of Zephyr Flight 80 so far, Frank?"

"One hundred and eighteen people killed. The plane was full. It exploded within a minute of taking off at three-ten this morning. The airlines people insist the plane was in perfect condition. They also insist there was no dangerous cargo aboard, but that is yet to be confirmed. Passengers went through a fully operational airport security check; nothing suspicious was reported. The cargo luggage check is a little more doubtful, as luggage was coming from four points of origin, Boston, Chicago, Atlanta, and San Francisco. The plane was blown to smithereens. I saw it."

"You saw it?"

"Yes."

For once, the sky in Boston had been perfectly clear, allowing him and his children to see one hundred and eighteen people blown apart, their parts burning, falling, falling through the sky.

"Almost all the evidence fell into Boston Harbor."

" 'Almost all'?"

"I found a severed human hand in my backyard this morning."

"I'll bet you said, 'Pull yourself together, Charlie.' I mean, when you found it."

"I think I did. To myself."

Priddy laughed. "I remember your saying that that time in San Matías. Do you remember? Bits of bodies everywhere—"

"Any laugh in a disaster," said Flynn. "Any laugh in a disaster. The worse the disaster, the worse the joke, I'm afraid."

"It keeps you from throwing up."

Priddy gave Flynn a quick, anxious glance.

"The story that the plane was shot down by a rocket fired from a submarine is being generally discounted," said Flynn. "I haven't looked into it myself."

Priddy said, "You might."

"Really?"

"Yes. It's not impossible."

"I gather not, if you and I are standing in this chilly place, talking. Did you have me assigned to this case?"

"Yes. Sorry, I couldn't get you on the phone earlier this morning. It's just a coincidence: you hiding out in the Boston Police Department while things cool down worldwide and a big bang like this comes along. Right man in the right place at the right time." As he walked, Priddy clapped his left shoe against his right. "Just as if I'd planned it."

"Right," said Flynn. "The only people on the passenger list causing any general conversation are a federal judge named Charles Fleming—who, incidentally, tried to take out five hundred thousand dollars' worth of flight insurance on himself before boarding—the actor, Daryl Conover, and the young man who won the World Middleweight Crown last night, Percy Leeper."

"Oh," Priddy said, "that's too bad. I didn't know that."

"None of the other names mean much to me, but that matters not at all. When you have one hundred and eighteen people murdered . . . what's the math of it, John Roy? In a group that size, how many potential suicides, murder victims, fanatics might there be?"

"Oh, not that many. The world's on a far more even keel than the facts ever lead us to believe."

"Say it so?"

"Our own lives, Frank, mustn't allow us to let our perceptions be distorted."

"Nevertheless, a mass murder such as this might easily come down to a stewardess with a rejected boyfriend."

"It might."

"The last thing is that the Human Surplus League has claimed credit for the explosion. They seem the usual sewer-type variety of nihilists. I've sent the sons in hot pursuit of them."

"Randy and Todd?"

"Yes."

"Great. The more experience they get, the better it is for everybody."

Flynn smiled. "It increases their options in life."

"Remember, Frank, after you did your bit in Nazi Germany as a teenager you turned away from the whole thing? Studied philosophy in Dublin."

"I had seen hell."

"And finally you turned away from it, and came back to us."

"I had had enough of truth." They walked a moment in silence.

Priddy said, "So what's your conclusion, Frank?"

"That a case like this most likely will take years and years to solve. That the chances of its ever getting into a court of law are exceedingly slim."

They turned around.

At the airplane, Grover and an Air Police sergeant were standing, fists on hips, noses within an inch of each other, faces beaming red in the increasing wetness of the day, shouting at each other furiously, simultaneously.

Grover was in his element. Nothing he liked better than a good nose-to-nose shouting match. He'd be more relaxed for days.

The other Air Policeman stood aside, hands also on hips, a white truncheon clutched in one hand.

The pilot of the modified F-100 had never appeared. The forward cockpit had remained closed.

"You missed something, Frank," Priddy said. "I'm really surprised."

"Where did I miss it?"

"On the passenger list."

Flynn said, "Then I'm still missing it, O wondrous chief of N. N. You'll have to enlighten me."

"Three men boarded that plane together, carrying American passports in the names of Abbott, Bartlett, and Carson."

"A, B, C," said Flynn. "Smith, Brown, and Jones. I detect the level of deception usually achieved only by the United States State Department."

"Yeah."

"Who were they?"

"Not 'they' so much as he. 'Abbott' was a body-guard; 'Carson' a bodyguard-secretary type; he, 'Bartlett,' was Rashin al Khatid, Ifadi Minister of the Exchequer."

"Ah!"

" 'Carson's' real name was Mihson Taha; 'Abbott's' was Nazim Salem Zoyad."

"What deception! They fooled us again."

"Somebody has fooled us."

"What were they doing here?"

"You must be short of sleep, Frank. What was the Minister of the Exchequer of the newly declared Republic of Ifad doing in Boston?"

"Banking."

"The story we have is that he was here to arrange, through one of these private, Boston international banks, the transfer of something like a quarter of a billion dollars' worth of gold into International Credits."

"What bank?"

"It's called Kassel-Winton."

"Never heard of it."

"Of course not. It's not one of your usual home-lending institutions. A very private, very international bank."

"Why the secrecy, John Roy? I don't get that at all."

"Frank, Arabians love long, loose robes. Burnooses and sunglasses. Walls around their houses. They keep their wives under their beds. You know all that."

"But what I do not know is why the United States State Department gave in to this sense of modesty and provided them with American passports."

"Two reasons, I think. The first is that Ifad has oil fields and United States policy is to be nice to people who have oil fields, however small. The second reason is that Ifad intends to use its quarter of a billion dollars of International Credits in purchasing American armaments."

"Of course," said Flynn. "I should have known."

66

"As you also should know, the average American tax-payer gets enraged every time he hears that his nation is providing armaments for everybody on every side of every quarrel, the world around."

"Purely defensive weapons," Flynn said, "I'm sure."

"Come on," said Priddy. "Let's walk back. I'm getting cold."

"Well," said Flynn. "So Rashin al Khatid, Minister of the Exchequer of the Republic of Ifad, was also murdered last night. What does it mean?"

"I don't know."

"Next we'll discover the President of the United States was aboard that plane last night, disguised in a wig and putty nose."

"No," said Priddy. "I saw him this morning."

"And how was he?"

"He didn't ask for you."

"An oversight, I'm sure."

Down the field, the sergeants' debate obviously remained unresolved. They leaned against their separate vehicles, sulking.

The truncheon had not been used on Grover.

"What do you need, Frank?"

"I need to see the top dogs at the bank. Kassel-Winton, is it?"

"It will be arranged."

"I want to see all of them. Everyone who knew about the Minister's visit and the nature of his visit."

"Okay. What else?"

"I don't know. This is an unexpected element."

"I don't think the Minister was expecting it, either."

"I daresay not. Does the FBI know about this?"

"Absolutely not. Can't have them creeping around, writing reports to each other."

Just before they arrived within hearing of the men by the plane, they stopped again.

"Try not to blow your cover, Frank. It's going to be difficult on this one."

"Did you ever see anyone who looks more like a Boston cop?"

"Yes," said Priddy. "And I've never been in Boston before. Do you enjoy the double salary?"

"It helps out."

"Still have the farm in Ireland?"

"Yes," said Flynn. "Near Loch Nafooie."

"You should get the kids over there," Priddy said. "For the summer."

"Maybe I will," said Flynn. "Thanks for the tea."

Nine

"No one home," Grover said.

Flynn rang the bell of The Meadows, Wood Lane, Kendall Green, himself.

It was the sort of farm cottage common to the South of France, low, long, wheat-colored stucco with well-placed, recessed windows and doors, at the end of a long gravel drive, surrounded by well-tended lawns and gardens.

"This place would be beautiful in the spring and summer," said Flynn.

Grover said, "This is how a judge lives. I've never known a judge to risk his life in the street."

"It's the sitting that makes him valuable," said Flynn. "The sitting-being-lied-to."

A small, pink motorcycle with a sidecar turned into the driveway, and crunched sedately along the gravel toward them.

The person driving the motorcycle wore a pink nylon, one-piece suit, pink helmet, and blue suede boots and gloves.

"Wait a minute," said Flynn. "I've got to see this. What could he be delivering? Flamingo eggs?"

The motorcycle stopped in front of the walk leading to the front door.

A pink knapsack was strapped to the person's back.

Remaining astride the motorcycle a moment, the person looked at them through plastic goggles.

Then the person put the plastic goggles on top of her helmet, took the helmet off and shook out her hair.

She said, "You're very quick, Inspector Flynn."

"And who might you be?"

The figure, feet flat on the ground forward of her, shoulders hunched, chin lowered, said, "Sassie Fleming."

"Sassie, is it?"

"I might be a widow," Sassie said. "I guess I am. I just heard."

"You're Judge Fleming's wife?" shouted Grover.

She measured him with her eyes.

"Widow Fleming," she said.

She got off the motorcycle and came up the walk.

"Bad news travels fast," she said. "I thought I'd have an hour or two to myself, before you arrived."

After she opened the front door to them and led them inside, she said, "Have you been waiting long?"

They said nothing.

Flynn watched her swing the knapsack off her back and dump it in a chair. She unzipped the nylon to just above her waist.

She turned to them, took a deep breath, hands on hips, and looked at Flynn evenly.

"Well—" she said.

There was a tiny green fleck in her left brown eye.

Her face was extremely white. Her chin quivered just slightly. Her mouth was dry.

She went between them and down a few steps into the living room. Immediately she was standing at a sliding glass door, looking into the garden.

Grover had out his notebook and pen.

"What's your full name?" he asked.

"Sarah Phillips Fleming, aka Sassie Phillips, aka Sassie Fleming, aka Mrs. Charles Fleming, also aka Ms. Phillips, Ms. Fleming, Doctor Phillips, Doctor Fleming."

She turned to them and continued: "Address? The Meadows, Wood Lane, Kendall Green, Massachusetts. White Caucasian female. Age? Thirty-one. U.S. Citizen? Yes. Occupation? Teacher. No distinguishing marks." Her eyes were becoming wet. "No previous arrests or convictions. Whereabouts at the time of the crime? Subject says she was at airport with husband until one-thirty in the morning, when she went home alone to bed."

"I must warn you—," Grover said.

"That anything I say may be held against me in court, etcetera ad Miranda." Tears were on her cheeks. "Will you excuse me a moment?"

Flynn said, "Of course."

A few minutes later, she returned to the room, saying, "I'm sorry. At the moment, I'm more surprised than anything else. We had such a happy time last night."

They had heard water run in a basin.

Her hair was brushed, and she had taken off her one-piece motorcycle suit.

She was dressed in slacks and a turtleneck sweater.

Flynn and Grover remained standing in the living room.

"Can I get you something?" she asked.

"Thank you, no," Flynn said.

"Have you had lunch? I haven't. I don't suppose I should have any sherry just now. Alcohol so accentuates a shock. Perhaps you'd have a good belt of whiskey for me."

"I've never used it," said Flynn. "And Grover doesn't deserve it."

She looked at Grover with a slight, friendly smile.

"You're Sergeant Whelan, aren't you?"

71

Grover was being charmed, although it was against all his natural instincts.

"Yes, ma'm."

"How are things over at the Old Records Building? Bit drafty, isn't it?"

Grover glanced at Flynn.

"You have Lieutenant Concannon working with you, too," Sassie said to Flynn. "Unofficially, of course."

"Do you know Lieutenant Concannon?" Flynn asked.

"I've talked to him on the phone. That man is a real thinker. Funny, the police. As soon as a man's body becomes damaged, they throw him away in retirement. Shows you what they think of the mind. I'm sorry, I haven't asked you to sit. I'd rather stand for the moment." Again she looked through the window at the late winter garden. "I do wish I could get out and scrub around in the earth this afternoon." When she looked at the seated Flynn again, her smile was back on her face. "At least I'm lucky in that they sent old Reluctant Flynn to arrest me. Isn't that right? 'Reluctant' Flynn?"

Flynn said, "How do you know us?"

"I'm a criminologist," Sassie said. "I teach at the Law School. I'm also a consultant for the Boston Police, the State Police, and the New York City Police."

"I see."

"In fact," Sassie said, "I've worked you into one of my lectures, Flynn."

"As an example of what—or shouldn't I ask?"

"As a man of no known police experience or training, who suddenly appears with a unique rank on a city police department and in a short period achieves one of the most astounding arrest-and-conviction records in history. What's your secret, Flynn?"

"I listen."

72

"I've been through your dossiers several times. There are pages and pages missing."

"Are there?"

"Someday will you fill me in on your mysterious past?"

"Possibly," said Flynn.

Grover said, "Mrs. Fleming, if we could have a few facts . . . ?"

"Of course. What do you want to know?" Abruptly, she sat down, palms flat on her thighs, eyes fixed on a particular section of the rug. "I arrived home at a little past six last night, riding the motorcycle from the train station. I had a glass of milk and some crackers. I packed Charlie's bag for him. Took a shower and changed. At about eight-thirty I drove into town in Charlie's Audi and picked him up at the courthouse. He was waiting on the sidewalk outside. He had had to stay in town while his secretary finished typing his speech."

"Where was your husband going?" Grover asked.

"More precisely," said Flynn, "why was he going to London?"

"Oh," Sassie said. "I should have told you that. Charlie's a federal judge. Was a federal judge. We'd done this book together, on the American penal system. Not just prison reform. The nature of punishment itself. Charlie's terribly bright. I mean, when a person commits a crime against society, what, ideally, should society do with him? Why is prison necessarily an answer?" She looked warily at Flynn. "Under the circumstances, it sounds like I'm pleading my own brief, doesn't it?"

"Go on," Flynn said.

"The book was published months ago. In America, it caused not a ripple. Nobody read it in this country. Only the *Law Journal* reviewed it. In England, the book attracted much notice. Bless the British: They read. Any-

73

way, one or both of us were invited on a ten-day speaking tour by an English law group interested in penology, and we decided Charlie should be the one to go. He was going to speak to the law group, lecture at Oxford, be on one of those television-panel things, you know. Something had been arranged for him in Cardiff, Edinburgh, Dublin."

"Why did you decide he should be the one to go?" asked Flynn.

"This is a busy time for me. No one could take over my classes at the University for me. I mean, a teacher does have times during the year to make such trips, and this isn't one of them. Yet this is the time the British law group had everything arranged. Besides that, Charlie needed a break in routine."

"Do I understand," said Flynn, "you encouraged your husband to take the trip, knowing you were not going with him?"

"I guess so."

"And you packed his bag for him?"

She said, "It looks bad, doesn't it? Obviously I put the dynamite, or the bomb, or whatever into his suitcase."

"Obviously," said Flynn.

"Oh, my."

"Is that an admission of guilt?" asked Grover.

"The lady made a pleasantry," said Flynn.

She said, "It wasn't a pleasantry, Inspector."

"An unpleasantry, then. What did you do after you picked up your husband?"

"We drove to Pier Four. You can park there, easily. We had a lovely dinner. Baked stuffed lobster. We had a couple of drinks before dinner. We had plenty of time. Plenty of wine. Charlie was in the mood of a schoolboy let off from school. And I think we were both happy our book was getting some attention. Do you understand?"

74

"I think so," said Flynn.

"We were tiddily, Inspector."

Grover said, "Tiddily?"

Sassie said, "Even a federal judge gets tiddily."

"I've often suspected it," said Flynn.

"We got to the airport sometime after twelve. Charlie checked in, checked his baggage through. Going down the corridor we came across one of those insurance machines. Well, I don't know if you can understand the rest of it."

"Try me," said Flynn.

"We had gotten into this teenage moony sort of mood. It had started by my saying I would miss him, and he said he'd miss me more than I missed him, and I said, Oh, no, I'd miss him more than he missed me. It was all rather silly. And then we came across this flight insurance machine. I said, 'I'll show you how much I'm going to miss you,' and paid for a five-thousand-dollar policy. He put on looking hurt, and took out twenty-five thousand dollars on himself. I took out fifty thousand dollars on him. It became competitive. I suppose it had something to do with the fact that we each have our own incomes. It's sort of a standing gag between us. You know, who pays for the petunias and who pays for the daffodils. We always end up with much more than we need of everything. Noisy people were shoving down the corridor behind us. And here we were, quietly playing this silly game in the corner. At this moment, I have no idea how much insurance we took out."

"Half a million," said Flynn.

"Half a million dollars?"

"Five hundred thousand dollars."

"My God. I didn't even remember we did this crazy thing until I was coming home on the train an hour ago. Oh, my God."

"Puts you in a difficult spot," said Flynn.

"That's why I wasn't all that surprised when I saw you at my front door when I got home just now."

"What time did you leave the airport?"

"Sometime after one. One-fifteen. One-thirty. Today was to be a workday for me, and Charlie had his mystery novel to read."

"The Judge read mystery novels?" asked Grover.

"He was an addict."

"Them things," said Grover.

"I came home in the car, had a glass of milk, went to bed. I was a little slow moving this morning. I slept late, gave myself breakfast, gathered up my things, rode the bike to the station, took the train into town. I planned to meet with my twelve o'clock class. I didn't know anything had happened. I said 'Hi' to Jim Burton in the corridor. He looked perplexed, turned around and came after me. He said, 'What are you doing here?' I said, 'Why?' He took me into the lounge and gave me a cup of coffee. I thought I'd had a reality separation. He told me about the air crash. Then he called the nurse over from the day clinic. She sat with me for a while. She didn't give me anything. I had to drive the bike home from the railway station, you see——"

Her voice faded away.

She took a tissue from her pocket.

"Poor old Charlie." She blew her nose. "Such a nice bag of bones."

Grover flipped his notebook back a few pages.

"Let's go over this——"

"Not now, Grover," interrupted Flynn. "Tell me, Mrs. Fleming, do you and your husband have children?"

"Charlie has a son, by his first wife. Charles Junior. Chicky. He's nearly as old as I am. He's twenty-six. Charlie's a good deal older than I am. His first wife died.

Of leukemia." She put the tissue in her pocket. "I'm going to take this," Sassie said. "If Charlie could take widowhood gracefully, I'm just going to have to."

"Did your husband have any other insurance you know of?" Flynn asked.

"I don't know. Yes. He had the sort of insurance that pays off your house mortgage if you die. Besides that, I guess he had some insurance as a federal employee. Whatever that would be. Not much. Charlie didn't need insurance. His son was grown up. We both had good incomes. That's why that game we were playing with the insurance machine last night was so stupid. So meaningless."

"I expect you'll get the policies in the mail," Flynn said. "In a day or two."

"I'll throw them away," she said.

Grover said, "Yeah."

"As far as you know, was your husband in good health, Mrs. Fleming?" Flynn asked.

"Yes. Perfect. In fact, he had his annual checkup a month ago. It was his joke that he always had a complete physical exam before doing anything about his income taxes. I saw the reports. He was in splendid condition for a man of fifty-three."

Flynn wondered if the hand he had found in his backyard that morning could possibly have been the hand of Judge Charles Fleming.

"Had he been depressed about anything lately?"

Grover scowled at this wrong question by Flynn.

"No. He was a little low Sunday, after Chicky left."

"His son?"

"Yes. Chicky came out Sunday. They took a walk in the woods together."

"What was your husband depressed about?"

"He didn't say."

"Where does Chicky live?"

"North side of Beacon Hill. Forster Street. Messy bachelor apartment."

"What does he do for a living?"

Her voice had slowed considerably.

"He's a pharmacist."

Again, Grover flipped back a few pages in his notebook.

"Let's go over this," he said firmly. "You encouraged your husband to fly alone to London last night. At six o'clock or thereabouts you came home and packed his suitcase for him. Did he ever open that suitcase?"

"No."

"You picked him up at his office, drove him to a restaurant, and got him drunk." Flynn winced. "You drove to the airport?"

"Yes."

"You waited at the airport with him until after you saw his luggage had been accepted for being put aboard the airplane."

"Yes."

"Then, either by yourself, or, in accordance with the story you told us, as some kind of a game you initiated with your inebriated husband, the Judge, you think you took out five hundred thousand dollars in flight insurance on his life."

She said, "So I understand."

"Immediately after doing this, you left him at the airport where he still had an hour or two to wait for his plane."

"That's right."

"Then you say you came home, went to bed by yourself—nobody can prove this—and got up this morning and went into town to act all innocent-pie. You didn't

78

listen to the radio, or television, or see a newspaper, or nothing?"

"No."

A pointed question was burning in Grover's brain.

"And your husband was twenty-two years older than you are?"

"Yes."

Grover was leaning forward like a goalie who spotted the puck ten feet away.

"Mrs. Fleming, who's your boyfriend?"

Her eyes grew wide as she stared at him.

Color appeared over her cheekbones.

She said nothing.

"More to the point," said Flynn, "your being a criminologist, I suspect you know the elements that go into the making of a bomb, and how to put them together?"

"It's not one of my specialties, Inspector."

"But you could do it, if you were pressed?"

"I suppose so."

"And in your work as a police consultant, you have easy access to the police laboratories where the makings of a bomb probably are available?"

"Yes. I suppose so." She looked up at him, sharply. "Shall I get my toothbrush?"

Flynn stood up.

"No."

"Inspector," Grover said.

"What is it now, Grover?"

"We have a perfectly good arrest here. She had motive, opportunity, method, access to the materials—"

"I'm sure you're right, Grover."

Her smile was sardonic. " 'Reluctant' Flynn."

"Inspector, I'm going to arrest her."

"We shall have no such firmness on your part, Grover."

79

"I am."

"You are not. You are going to drive me back to the Old Records Building."

Grover slapped his pen down hard on the cover of his notebook.

"Why?"

"Because," said Flynn, "Cocky moved his Bishop. I just figured out what to do about it."

Ten

He moved his Knight to King Bishop Three.

On his desk, along with several notes, each typed on its own piece of paper, was a map of Boston with red dots carefully marked on it, concentrated in the northeast of Boston. A half-dozen dots had blue circles around them.

That was Cocky's doing.

"You'd better get over to Harvard Square now," Flynn said to Grover, "to arrest my sons."

"I don't want to do that," Grover said.

"Any time you wish to request a transfer," Flynn said, "I will sign the application happily. Several times. In a large hand."

"I request a transfer five times a week. Six, if I work on Saturdays."

"Pity none of them take hold. By the way, what did you tell the Air Police out at Hanscom Field?"

The trip from there to Kendall Green had been in stony silence.

"I told them you were a Boston Police Inspector, and they could ask you what the hell you were doing there themselves."

"They never did. Are you sure that's all you said?"

"What were we doing there, anyway?"

"Picking up some tea. Papaya Mint." Flynn took it

81

from his pocket. "Must tell Cocky I have it. A cup wouldn't be bad now."

Flynn picked up the receiver of the ringing phone.

"Off with you now, Sergeant Whelan. Go do what you like best. Try to arrest someone."

Into the phone, he said, "Hello?"

"Flynn?"

"Flynn it is," said Flynn, settling into his deep desk chair. "Francis Xavier, as my mother would have it."

"Jesus Christ, don't you even know how to answer a phone?"

"I think I do," said Flynn. "You pick up the lighter of the two parts of the instrument, the one on top, stick one end against the ear, bring the other end close to the mouth, and make an anticipatory noise into it, politely if possible. Have I got it right?"

"You should identify yourself. Crisply."

"You mean, I should answer saying, 'Inspector Flynn here'?"

"Right!"

"But if you don't know whom you're calling," Flynn said, "why should I give you the satisfaction of telling you to whom you're talking? Answer me that, now."

"This is Hess."

"Hess?"

"FBI."

"FBI?"

"Federal Bureau of Investigation, Goddamn it!"

"Ah, the Fibby. You should have said so."

"Where the hell were you this afternoon?"

"Taking a ride in the country. We don't get such clear weather so often in Boston we can afford to squander it frivolously."

"Jesus, are you serious?"

"In fact, I think it's turning nasty again at the moment. Fearful-looking clouds were coming in from the East—"

"I didn't call you for a weather report!"

"Too bad," said Flynn. "I'm rather good at it."

"You've been assigned to work with us. Where's our ground transportation?"

"Let me think now. On the ground, would it be?"

"What hotel have you put us in?"

"I haven't put you in any hotel, but I have a man at this very moment standing on line to get you some opera tickets. They're doing Wagner's *Götterdämmerung* tonight, and I knew that would pep you up—"

Cocky had come in, spotted the package of Papaya Mint tea on the desk, and carried it away with him.

"Jesus Christ, all you local yokels are alike. Can't get you out of the local bars."

"Tell me," said Flynn, "what are you boyos doing about the HSL?"

"The who?"

"The Human Surplus League," said Flynn, "who, I still maintain, may have a point, if they let me do their selecting for them."

"You know about them?"

"I heard a rumor."

The afternoon *Star* was on his desk, opened to their statement.

"We've got a dozen men on their trail."

"And how would they be going about it?"

"Basic police work, Flynn! They're asking around."

"Ah! Is that how it's done? May the moon shine on their efforts. Any other leads?"

"No."

"Is that the truth, now?"

"As far as you're concerned."

"What about the boyo in Dorchester who believes he saw the aircraft shot down by a rocket?"

"That's in a class with the rest of you Boston drunks."

"Not paying any heed to that one?"

83

"Of course not. Flynn, you get your ass over here to Logan Airport as fast as you can travel. You hear me?"

"A little cooperation is what you're asking for, is that it?"

"Report in to me personally. Immediately. Or I'll have your ass in a sling!"

"I expect it would be cumbersome, to say the least, toting about such a thing."

"You heard me!"

"This is Inspector Francis Xavier Flynn," Flynn said, "hanging up."

Flynn sat at his desk, reading Cocky's notes.

The first read: "Insp.—Three men got on that airplane this morning, together, named Abbott, Bartlett, & Carson. A-B-C. Susp.? U.S. passports."

Flynn crumpled that note up and threw it in the wastebasket.

The second read: "Insp.—Producer of show at Colonial, *Hamlet,* name of Baird Hastings, was trained by U.S. Army as a demolition expert. Trouble between him and star Daryl Conover unknown, but apparently Conover walked out on the show last night."

"Hurumph," Flynn muttered. "No end of difficulties here."

Then he read the statement in the afternoon *Star* issued by the Human Surplus League: "We, the people of the Human Surplus League, in order to reform a more perfect Union, reestablish Justice, reinsure domestic Tranquility, provide for the common defense of the World in the Universe, promote the general Welfare, and secure the Blessing of Liberty to ourselves and our Posterity, do declare that we have commenced a campaign of mass murder, in the exploding of the passenger airplane to London this morning, killing one hundred and eighteen people.

84

"We appeal to all right-thinking people to conjoin with us in a campaign of mass murder, seizing every opportunity available to the individual or the group to annihilate, by their own mechanical devices, as many of their fellow persons as is humanly possible.

"The World is running out of food, space, air, fuel, fresh water. Population density causes people to be in conflict with each other increasingly. As our natural resources diminish, competition for them must increase through wars and other acts of hatred. Union is impossible. Prisons are overcrowded; Courts are delayed years in hearing cases because of the jam: Justice is impossible. The Earth, crawling with so many people, is militarily indefensible in the event of attack from Outer Space. There can be no Liberty for ourselves or our Posterity; there can be no domestic Tranquility; there can be no general Welfare if the world is such that no one has room to move!

"Therefore, We say to you, let us embark, without hatred, while there is still time to do so lovingly, upon a program of continuous mass murder!

"Our program:

"1. Wherever two or more are gathered together, murder them.

"2. Destroy hospitals, medical schools, and other life-support systems.

"3. Encourage the natural proclivities of our politicians to wage war, especially thermonuclear war.

"4. Promote the carrying of personal concealed weapons; incite riots; encourage civil insurrection.

"5. Germinate your fellow person with as many diseases, especially fatal, at your disposal as you can.

"6. In your loving killing, be without class, racial, religious, or ethnic bias: kill generally, without prejudice.

"Remember our Motto: Do the World A Favor—Drop Dead."

"Ah, the little darlings," Flynn said as Cocky came in the door carrying the small tea tray. "Just the reading you want with a nice cup of Papaya Mint tea. Their parents are proud to have brought them into the world, I'm sure."

Next to the article was the headline: BUSINESS LEADERS RESIST HSL MESSAGE—*Fear Concert, Theater Business Off—Religious Leaders Scorn Group*.

Flynn had a sip of his tea while Cocky went to the chessboard.

"That's the old stuff. Up the nose it goes. Now, what else do we have here?"

"Insp.—I talked to Paul Levitt, sportswriter for the *Herald-American*. Says Marion 'Forker' Henry, who lost World Middleweight Crown to Percy Leeper last night, is not such a good boxer, although rated number one in this country. Nickname is not really 'Forker,' but that's how it is spelled in newspapers. Suspects Mafia jockeyed him into number one position, a lot of money has been invested in him, and suggests Forker's manager, Alf Walbridge, be investigated. Did not discount possibility Leeper was paid off to throw fight and then didn't do so. Might explain his leaving the country so soon after the fight."

"Ah, Cocky," said Flynn, "you're percolating today. And not a word to you!"

"Insp.—Thought occurs to me there was plenty of time to make and put aboard that airplane this morning a bomb by anyone involved with either Daryl Conover (Curtain time: 10:48) or Percy Leeper (boxing match was called at 11:03), as long as they had the materials. The mob has. Would a theater producer?"

The last note read: "Insp.—Checked with Beverly police. Producer Baird Hastings (who changed his name from Robert Cullen Hastings, known as "Bob" Hastings in the Army) has taken out a license to buy dynamite to blast out a rock ledge behind his house in Beverly Farms."

"Good work, Cocky! The man's a genius! And the tea's not bad, either."

Flynn put Cocky's map in his pocket.

"If anyone inquires for me, tell them I'm wending my way home by subway and bus, and will mark the grave of anyone who dares call me tonight."

Cocky answered the phone.

"Meantime," continued Flynn, "you can figure out what to do with your imperiled Rook."

Mouthpiece pressed against his left shoulder, Cocky said, "Inspector Hess, FBI."

"Him," Flynn said from the door, "you can tell I've stepped down to the corner for a wee dram, and good night!"

Eleven

"Dreadful big matters involved here," said Flynn as he pulled off a sock.

He had already told Elsbeth everything, including N. N. and the Ifadi Minister of the Exchequer.

In bed, she opened her Robinson's *Medieval and Modern Times*.

"The more you chase big matters," said Elsbeth, "the more likely it is to be some little schnook scared of dying alone." She turned the page. "Come to bed."

Twelve

Hearing the front door open caused Flynn to call out from the dining room, "Are you going to appear with the toast every morning?"

Grover stood in the doorway.

"What on earth happened to you?" asked Elsbeth.

Grover said, "I have received orders to bring you to Logan Airport, Inspector. Hangar D."

"Whose orders?"

"Captain Reagan's, sir. Speaking for the Commissioner."

"Hess," said Flynn.

"What happened to you?" Elsbeth asked.

Grover's right eye was closed and purple. He had a red welt on his left cheekbone. The right side of his upper and lower lips was puffed and red.

Grover said nothing.

"Some coffee, Sergeant?" Elsbeth asked. "Jenny, get the Sergeant a cup."

"I wouldn't drink coffee in this house—"

"Come, come now, Grover," began Flynn.

"Your sons did this to me!" Grover pointed dramatically at Elsbeth's head. "Your Goddamned brats! I'm gonna kill 'em!"

"Such language, Sergeant," said Elsbeth.

"I swear, I'm gonna kill 'em. I'm gonna beat the shit out of them. One by one."

"You can't beat them together," said Flynn, "I take it."

"Okay, so I grab for both of them when they come out of the subway, over at Harvard Square. I shout at them. I identify myself as a police officer. They run through four lanes of traffic across the street. Push through crowds of decent people the other side of the street. Knock a professor-type on his ass. One goes left; the other one goes right. I commence chasing the one that goes left."

"The one you had the greater chance of catching," observed Flynn. "Must have tripped over something."

"I catch the little bastard outside the Paperback Booksmith. Slam his head into the corner of the door. Grab his hands behind his back. I almost get the cuffs on him but the Goddamned knapsack kept gettin' in the way. A big crowd gathers, everybody watchin', sayin' 'Boo!,' shoutin' 'Leave the kid alone!' I identify myself as a police officer. Suddenly, the other one appears from nowhere, hits me sideways, lands on my back, knockin' me off balance. Once I'm spun around, he belts me in the face. I still had grab ahold the wrist of one of them. He belts me the other side of the face. I fall back against this table they got books out on for sale. It smashes against the store window. Behind me, I hear the big, plate-glass store window coming down. I goes, 'I'm a police officer, Goddamn it!' They began to get away. Bouncin' off the table, I grab ahold one of their knapsacks. Suddenly, the other one whips around and butts me in the stomach with his head like a goat. With the window comin' down behind me and all, I had to let go of the knapsack. Then that one whips around and gets me in the mouth with the back of his hand, sendin' me sideways." Grover touched his lip gently. "If I had fallen straight back, I could have got decapitated!"

Winny, over his scrambled egg, said, "Wow!"

"They got away?" asked Flynn.

"The little bastards." Grover's dark look at Elsbeth was purposeful.

"They weren't hurt?" asked Elsbeth.

"They're gonna be!"

"What happened then?" asked Winny.

"The manager come out of the store, purple-faced, fists all ready to go. I figure the crowd will calm down faster if I remain sittin' on the sidewalk. They're hurling imprecations at me. The little bastards are nowhere to be seen. They disappeared like the crowd swallowed them, instead of anybody comin' to the aid of an officer in distress. The manager, he's screamin' at me.

"I identify myself as a police officer.

"Then two of these Cambridge cops come amblin' up, swingin' their nightsticks, blue suiters just as shitty as they come. 'He's no cop,' they says to the manager. 'We never saw him before.' So I shows 'em my Boston Police badge. 'I'm a Sergeant in the Boston Police,' I says. 'Oh, you're a Boston Policeman,' they say, makin' a big thing out of it. 'Then what are you doin' operatin' in Cambridge? What would your boss say if he knew you were operating in Cambridge?' Still sittin' there, glass all around, I shouts, 'My boss is Inspector Flynn, the God-damned nut, and you can talk to him about it.' "

"They never did," said Flynn.

" 'Inspector Flynn?' goes one. 'Tell us another. Over here in Cambridge we don't believe any such man exists.' "

Still standing in the doorway of the dining room, Grover looked tired and dejected, hands loose at his sides.

After a moment, he shook his head slowly.

His lips moved, soundlessly.

"Poor Grover." Jenny dusted the toast crumbs from her fingers.

Flynn said, "Grover, having listened to you just now, I can say I think you missed part of the point. You were supposed to pretend to be arresting them. Your effort wasn't supposed to be successful. If you were really trying to get the handcuffs on one of them, you were going a bit too far. You caused yourself more grief than you needed."

"I figured if I got one of them—" Grover lowered his head again.

"—You'd end up lookin' better to the crowd; your pride would be intact," concluded Flynn. "That wasn't the point! I wanted both of them working!"

"Well, they are, Da," said Jenny reasonably.

"It's just that Sergeant Whelan got bopped," added Winny. "Good and bopped."

Standing up from the table, Flynn said, "He got nothing less than he deserved."

"I really am sorry, Sergeant," said Elsbeth. "My sons are so vigorous. They're a handful for anybody!"

"Ah, the darling boys." Flynn was putting on his overcoat. "And to think, I raised them myself!"

Thirteen

In the huge, gloomy, freezing airport hangar, Hess fixed Flynn with a sideways, bloodshot eye.

"Where's your stupid sidekick?"

"I ordered him home," said Flynn, "for a sick day. He took a bit of a thumping last night—in the line of duty, of course—and was so full of resentment and smarts I didn't think he should have to work the day. That, and all the stopping and waiting outside pawnshops I've had him do, has gotten him demoralized, it all has."

"Pawnshops?" Hess asked absently. "What've pawnshops got to do with it?"

"Yes," said Flynn. "We stopped at three or four on the way in, just a quick look in each one, you know. I looked at as many on my way home last night. So far, no luck. You'd be surprised how many pawnshops there are in the world."

"Double-talk," Hess said. "Interpreted loosely, you and your idiot guardian tied one on last night, and you could get up this morning, and he couldn't."

"Oh?" said Flynn. "And were we with you last night?"

"You were not," said Hess, moving closer to the assembled group of Fibbies and Cabs. Hess's mild manner may have been because he had been standing separated from the group when Flynn entered. And Flynn, a foot taller and considerably broader in the shoulder, had stood between the group and Hess, very close to him. And said nothing. "You certainly weren't."

Baumberg was clearing his throat.

The hangar was strewn with pieces of Zephyr Flight 80 to London.

The tail section, almost intact, chewed off just aft of the coach galley, looked more of the sea than of the air: a leviathan, its radio antenna still giving it a look of forward movement.

The front of the airplane had been twisted off, again at about where the forward galley was. Flynn peered into the charred tunnel. Men with lights on extension cords were working on the instrument panel.

A row of double seats, which Baumberg said were from the first-class, port-side section, were intact, the upholstery saltwater-soaked. Each seat belt had been cut. The bodies had been removed.

Apparently the people in these seats, attached to their seats, attached to each other, had ridden down the sky together to the sea.

Sections of both wings had been found; only three of the four engines; other large and small pieces of the airplane lay about, not yet in any order.

"For anyone who doesn't know already," Baumberg was trying to be heard in the hangar, "we are now reasonably certain this aircraft was blown up by a bomb in a suitcase situated in the rear starboard luggage hold."

"What do you mean, 'reasonably certain'?" said Hess.

"Well," said Baumberg, "we still haven't found the other starboard engine. Nothing definite should be said until we do. Especially as that engine was on the side the explosion took place."

"You mean," began young Ransay, slowly, "that it is

possible that one of the starboard engines could have caused the explosion?"

"Not really," said Baumberg.

Ransay said, "How? You mean, some element in the engine could have blown up, fallen back into the cargo hold, and blown up again?"

"No." Baumberg's eyes were so tired they were devoid of expression. "I don't know what I'm saying. We have evidence, as you've seen, that an explosion happened from within the rear starboard luggage hold. The metal around that cargo hold received the major, outward-blowing impact of the explosion. All the other evidence indicates the blow originated from that place and only that place, both by direction and quality of impact."

"Then why are you talking about the engine?" asked Ransay.

"Because we haven't found it yet," answered Baumberg. "I guess I'm being academic."

"You're being stupid," said Hess.

Baumberg's face turned slowly, tiredly, to anger.

"Mister Baumberg," said Flynn. "Do we know yet what the rest of the cargo was?"

"We know, Flynn!" shouted Hess. "The rest of us know. The rest of us who have been working on this case!"

"Would anybody be good enough to share such knowledge with me?" Flynn patiently asked the hangar at large.

"Mail, Flynn! Mail!" screamed Hess.

"I see," said Flynn. "Anything else?"

Baumberg tried to smile. "There was also a shipment of experimental condoms. On their way to India."

"Condoms?" asked Flynn.

"Prophylactics."

"My, my," said Flynn. "If only the Human Surplus

95

League had known. In what way were they experimental?"

Tired, not realizing fully what he was saying, Baumberg said, "I can assure you there was nothing explosive in them."

Everyone had a great laugh.

Baumberg, when he realized what he had said, went into an uncontrollable giggling fit. The man was very near the edge of nervous exhaustion, clearly.

"Mister Baumberg," Flynn said, finally. "Is there any way anyone not traveling aboard that airplane could have gotten a piece of luggage, containing the bomb, into that luggage hold?"

"Of course," said Ransay. "He could have given it—he could have put it into the suitcase of someone who was traveling."

"Or," said Flynn, "it could have been put aboard by one of the luggage handlers."

Baumberg said, quickly, "That's possible."

"Or," said Flynn, "someone who had absolutely nothing to do with the airlines, the airport, or the airplane, could have ambled out to the field anytime between midnight and two o'clock, two-thirty, and stuffed that bomb aboard the airplane? You said that cargo hold had been left opened?"

"No," said Baumberg. "It wasn't left wide open. Of course not."

"Anyone," continued Flynn, "could conceivably have access to it?"

"Well, I suppose so. But airport security—"

"Is airport security really that tight?" asked Flynn.

"No. I suppose not."

"Another thing," said Flynn. "You were going to check to see if any of that luggage raised suspicion?"

"Yes," said Baumberg. "None did. You must realize

that most of the luggage had come from other parts of the country by plane. Presumably, people had already looked at it. For example, the luggage from the San Francisco plane was late. It was trucked straight across from one plane to another. It never entered the building. It was dark. It was two o'clock in the morning. Human psychology—"

"And the luggage originating in Boston?" asked Flynn.

"Nothing in it raised suspicion."

"Was it electronically scanned?" asked Flynn.

Baumberg, now, was sweating in the freezing hangar.

"Human psychology being as it is," said Baumberg. "You see, the other luggage, particularly the stuff from San Francisco, well, that wasn't scanned—"

"So the luggage from Boston wasn't either?"

Baumberg swallowed. "No."

"So actually none of the luggage here in Boston went through any kind of security?"

"Not here in Boston. It was looked at, of course, by the man who tickets the luggage. He's trained to make a personal appraisal of the traveler, of the luggage. If the traveler seems nervous or odd in any way, unduly concerned about his luggage; if the luggage itself seems too light, or too heavy—"

"—or if it's ticking," said a Cab.

"—then the luggage man marks that piece of luggage for a special scan, and he sees that it gets it. I repeat that none of the luggage going aboard Flight 80 raised even the slightest suspicion. You see, the luggage was examined, in a way—"

"But none of it was opened or electronically scanned," said Jack Rondell.

"Well, now, opening luggage," said Baumberg. "Customers don't like that too much. We'd need keys, permission."

"The luggage would have to be opened anyway in London," said Hess. "Go through Customs."

"That's another matter," answered Baumberg. "Customs is a governmental authority. If they say, 'Open your luggage,' you open your luggage. We're a private airline. We're not dealing with citizens, or aliens. We're dealing with customers. Human psychology—"

"Professor Baumberg!" shouted Hess. "Would you believe we have no Goddamned interest in your version of human psychology?"

Rondell looked mildly at Hess, and smiled.

"I guess we can thank you now, Mister Baumberg," said Rondell. "We now know fairly certainly the plane was blown up by something, most likely in a piece of luggage, put in the right, rear cargo hatch in Boston. Our own investigation indicates the bomb was most likely a lot of dynamite—what quantity, we don't know —most likely, as the explosion took place so soon after takeoff, ignited by radio, either from the plane, or from the earth."

"Is that so?" said Flynn.

"Yes, Inspector. It's our best guess. Most likely a time bomb wouldn't have gone off so soon. If you're going to use a time bomb, obviously you wouldn't take the chance of setting it for the minute after scheduled takeoff. How many planes actually take off on time? With the likelihood of a delayed departure, especially at this time of year, late winter, you might find yourself blowing up an empty airplane sitting on the runway."

"I see," said Flynn.

"Furthermore," continued Rondell, "it's a good guess the bomb was set off from the ground, rather than from inside the airplane. Supposing you're sitting there in the airplane, a passenger, with a radio switch in your pocket which can blow up the plane, and yourself. Would you press that button immediately on takeoff?"

Flynn said, "I think I might have a cup of tea, first."

"However, a person on the ground with a radio transmitter has got to press that switch before the plane gets out of range."

"What would be the range of such a toy as this?" asked Flynn.

" 'Toy'!" said Hess.

"Probably about seven miles."

Baumberg said, "I think we can be almost perfectly sure no one got aboard that airplane with a radio transmitter in his pocket. That would never have passed airport security."

"You can disguise a radio transmitter like this as anything. It could look like a hearing aid."

Baumberg said, "Oh."

Flynn said, "What you're saying is, that most likely this airplane was blown up by someone here at Logan Airport, standing at a window, watching it take off?"

"Speculation, Inspector," said Rondell. "But that's where our speculation has led us."

"Surely there aren't all that many people around an airport at three o'clock in the morning?"

"Not many," said Ransay. "But some."

"Inspector, as you would know, if you had been more cooperative with us," Rondell went on politely, "we are checking airport personnel who were on duty at that hour yesterday morning, to see if they saw or remember anyone acting strangely or suspiciously."

"So far nothing?"

"So far nothing."

"Why are we telling him all this?" Hess asked Rondell. "All the son of a bitch does is take rides in the country and hit the taverns!"

"Because." Rondell smiled with closed teeth at Flynn. "Because the Inspector is going to be a great help to us, from now on. Aren't you, Inspector?"

"Ach," said Flynn. " 'When there's constabulary work to be done, The constable's lot is a terrible one.' Have I got the line exactly right? I doubt it. I'll go look it up, I will."

Fourteen

"I rather like that Nathan Baumberg," Flynn said to the perfectly shaven, combed, polished, creased Paul Kirkman in the Passenger Services offices of Zephyr Airways. "But I'm not sure why he's taking the matter so much to heart."

Kirkman shook his head. "Nate's a great guy. Totally conscientious. Best in the business. Also a good friend. But you're right. He's taking this too personally. Too afraid the explosion might be proven his responsibility."

"Could it have been?"

"No way. Maintenance has checked out perfectly. Some kook put a bomb aboard that airplane, Inspector."

"It seems so."

"For my own sake, I had to decide, 'Okay, if I slipped up somewhere, let some mad bomber aboard that airplane, I get fired. My life isn't over.' The world is full of kooks. History has shown we can't identify and control them all."

"Madmen can be the most normal-looking people," said Flynn. "It's a part of their madness."

"Of course, Nate's got kids. I can pick up and move anywhere, anytime. Truth is, Inspector, we'll probably both be fired once this thing calms down a little. Our names will be identified with this air explosion for the

101

rest of our lives—at least in the industry. I can work anywhere, at anything. Nate's whole training is in aircraft."

Flynn cradled the bowl of his unlit pipe in both hands.

"Is there any way Baumberg could be responsible for the explosion?"

Kirkman looked blankly at Flynn.

"I mean, he would have had access to the plane. He's an engineer. He would know how to make a bomb. No one would ever notice him walking around the building with a hand-held radio transmitter. You use walkie-talkies often at airports. He would be able to see the airplane taking off—"

"I didn't see him, Inspector. As far as I know, he was at home asleep."

"You wouldn't have to see him. He must know this airport as well as he knows anything. He's a bright man."

"Nate Baumberg is no madman, Inspector."

"Ach, well. I'm sure you're right. And I'm sure his highly nervous reaction is entirely understandable, under the circumstances."

"Take it from me, Inspector. Nate Baumberg is simply a sincere, good man. I'm not saying he wouldn't hurt a fly, exactly. At one time he talked a lot about the Jewish Defense League."

"Did he, indeed?"

"Sort of surprised me at the time, but understandable when you think about it. His grandparents and the families of two uncles were wiped out by the Holocaust."

"Entirely understandable."

"He's told me he's contributed to the League. Now, understand, I'm not talking about his propensity to violence—which I believe is nearly nil. I believe he left the League when the stories about their nondefensive violence got around. I'm talking about his sincerity. Nate cares. As a person. He feels intensely."

"Did he ever actually tell you that he's left the League?"

"Inspector, whether or not Nate is a member of the Jewish Defense League is irrelevant. There was no high, Arabian muckety-muck aboard that airplane—no enemy to the State of Israel, or to the Jewish people. I merely stated his interest in the JDL as an example of how deeply Nate cares about things."

"But he's never told you he's no longer a member of the JDL?"

Kirkman said, "He hasn't mentioned it lately. I mean, in years."

Flynn stirred the ashes in his bowl.

"What I need from you, Mister Kirkman, is the assurance that everyone who was supposed to be aboard that airplane was aboard it."

"What do you mean, 'supposed to be'?"

"You've issued a list of names. One hundred and ten passengers: forty-eight in first class; sixty-two in coach; eight crew members. How do we know they were all aboard?"

"That's a strange question, Inspector."

"Is it?"

"Well, yeah. I mean, the passenger list has been out for twenty-four hours. All the newspapers have published it. Don't you think that if someone who was supposed to be aboard that airplane wasn't, he would have stood up by now and said, 'Hey, I'm alive'?"

"Yes," said Flynn. "I would."

"Then I don't get the question."

"Conversely, supposing someone were aboard that airplane you didn't expect to be aboard, and twenty-

103

four hours later no one admits to the fact—wouldn't you find that odd?"

"You mean a stowaway? There were no stowaways on Flight 80 to London."

"Something other than that. Supposing at the last minute, say, a stewardess got attacked by a bad case of the flu, or love, or something, and got a friend to substitute for her. Would you know it?"

"Of course. Those situations have to be reported. Absolutely."

"I'm afraid my example isn't much good."

"Inspector, have you ever flown?"

"A little."

"I mean, transatlantic. Have you been on a flight out of the country?"

"Once or twice."

"Then you should know the routine. Let me explain. If you're flying from one city in this country to another, you can use any name you want, legally, as long as you pay cash. You can say your name is Abraham Lincoln and fly from here to Atlanta, Georgia, and no one has the right to say 'Boo' at you. Of course, if you say your name is Abraham Lincoln and try to write a check or a credit slip in the name of Jefferson Davis, that might raise suspicions."

"Only might," said Flynn. "Only might, the American sense of credit being as slippery as it is."

"If you're flying out of the country, okay, so listen to me. You come into the terminal. Our man takes your baggage. You present to him your passenger ticket. He weighs your baggage. From your ticket, he makes out a route ticket for the baggage. He writes on the ticket where it is going, and on what flight. You are required to have your own tags on your luggage, stating your own name and address. He is supposed to check that name against the name on your ticket, to

104

make sure they match. If you have not provided tags for your bags, he will provide them for you, again checking what you say your name is against the name on the ticket."

"But the baggage doesn't get opened, does it?"

"No. If the man accepting the baggage thinks there's anything suspicious about the bag, or the person traveling, then he calls me. No one called me for Flight 80. I dropped by the counter once or twice."

"Sometimes people check in baggage for each other," said Flynn. "A father, or a mother, for a whole family. A travel escort—"

"There was nothing suspicious about anyone on Flight 80. Okay, so then the passengers go down the corridor toward their gate. They and their carry-on luggage go through a complete electronic scan. If there is anything suspicious about them or their luggage, they are thoroughly searched at that point. We can examine the carry-on luggage at that point, because the State Police are standing right there. That's why I'm sure this theory of the FBI is crazy. No one could have boarded Flight 80 with a radio transmitter without getting stopped."

"They suggest it wouldn't have looked like a radio transmitter," said Flynn. "It might have looked like a hearing aid."

Kirkman said, "Jesus."

"One can't keep up with the criminal mind," said Flynn. "Especially when it belongs to the FBI."

"All right. Then the passengers come to a stand-up desk. There they present their tickets and their passports. Our representative is supposed to see that the pictures they see on the passports are the same faces they see standing in front of them, and that the name on the passport is the same as the name on the ticket. He tears a slip from the ticket, with the passenger's

105

name on it. He gives the passenger a boarding pass, assigning a seat to him. Now, Inspector, the slips from all the tickets for all the passengers were picked up at that desk for Flight 80 Tuesday morning. All of them."

"Righto. You can make a specific seat reservation before that, can't you?"

"Yeah. A lot do. When they buy the tickets, or when they first come into the terminal. You know, people traveling together. Want to sit together. That sort of thing. Some people think it's safer to sit in front of the wings, others think behind the wings is safer. Others want to sit nearest the johns."

"People other than passengers go through the electronic control and down to the arrival-and-departure gates," asserted Flynn.

"They're not supposed to, but they do."

"People never do what they're supposed to do," noted Flynn. "Curse the lot of them."

"Boarding passes are taken from the passengers at either one of two places: the stewardess takes them aboard the airplane, as they come through the door; or a steward stands in the terminal at the entrance of the jetway and takes them."

"If the stewardess takes them, does she then fly away to London with them?"

"No. She hands them to the steward before the door is closed."

"Which place were the boarding passes picked up on this flight?"

"I'm not certain, but I expect at the entrance to the jetway. The stewardesses would probably be too busy. People are apt to be fussier on a transatlantic flight, especially at that hour of the morning."

"So the stewardesses wouldn't have seen the boarding passes on this flight, most likely?"

"Most likely not."

"Then is there a head-count aboard the plane? Sometimes I've noticed that."

"Not on this one. The feeder flights were in plenty of time. The point I'm trying to make, Inspector, is that we have all the boarding passes for Flight 80. All one hundred and ten of them."

"No head-count."

"All the boarding passes are all the boarding passes, Inspector."

"A definitive statement, that. Now, then, Mister Kirkman, only one more question. You've said several times you were around the airport that night, on duty, as it were, while Flight 80 was boarding and taking off."

"I'll never forget. In my job, you know, when one of your airplanes is taking off, you take a deep breath; your whole body relaxes. I was just doing that, starting back to my office, when I heard the bang."

"And a very considerable bang it was," said Flynn.

"If I didn't drop dead at that moment," said Kirkman, "I never will."

"You should never make such promises to yourself," said Flynn. "They may prove to be false. But tell me, did you happen to notice three men traveling together, probably formally dressed, you know, in dark business suits, maybe looking like foreigners to you, names of Bartlett, Carson, and Abbott?"

Kirkman looked at the passenger list on his desk. "Abbott, Bartlett, and Carson appear to have been traveling together. But they're not foreigners."

"I know. But did you happen to notice them?"

"If you ask me, I say, yes. I seem to have an impression of three men in dark suits, being quiet, sort of taking to the side of the waiting lounge there at Gate 18, you know, shirking, shrinking away from the other

107

passengers—especially after the passengers from San Francisco came in."

"Why especially the San Francisco passengers?"

"Well, they were on a theater-junket to London, you know, off on a holiday, they all knew each other, they'd had their drinks. Then they found Daryl Conover, the great English actor, would be boarding the plane with them, and they went through the roof with giddiness. Nobody did anything really wrong. They just gave him the big celebrity treatment."

"And how did the big celebrity respond?"

"Well, he wasn't exactly nasty. At first, he looked sort of angry. Then he said something like, 'I'm very tired. Would you please go away?' They kept it up. Then he asked the steward if he would show him to his first-class seat immediately."

"You mean, put him aboard the plane before anyone else?"

"Yes."

"And did you?"

"Yes. I did myself. Aboard, he grumbled a little bit, saying we should have done so sooner. He was right. We should have. You know, in Passenger Services, we have to respect people who are famous. Other people bother them. They have their rights to be left alone. Usually, though, such people as Daryl Conover get put aboard straight from the VIP lounge, so there's no problem for them, or us."

"Why wasn't Conover put aboard early, then?"

"I don't know. I guess he arrived a little late, and came straight to the gate."

"He had his ticket ahead of time?"

"No. He picked his ticket up in the main terminal. I saw him."

"And what about Percy Leeper?"

"I don't know who Percy Leeper is."

"He's the middleweight boxing champion of the world. As of last Monday night."

"Oh, is that who he was? There sure was a boxer going aboard. Tape over one eyebrow, still bleeding, mashed nose. That was Percy Leeper, uh? I thought we were going to have trouble with him."

"Why?"

"Oh, he was as high as a kite."

"Drunk?"

"No. I thought so at first. We had to take a can of beer away from him, before he boarded. No, he was just jumpin' around. He couldn't keep his feet still. He was doing little dances, drinking his beer, kept hugging the shoulders of the guy who was with him."

"You took a can of beer away from the boyo who just won the World Middleweight Boxing Championship?"

Kirkman chuckled. "Something to brag about, uh? If I had known who he was, maybe I would have thought twice."

"How drunk was he?"

"I don't think he was drunk at all. Or not very. Exuberant. He was perfectly nice about letting me take the beer can from him. He said something weird. What did he say? Some weird word. I know what he said. He put his hand on my arm and said, 'I'm just feeling peppermint.'"

"Peppy? Pepped-up?"

"No. He said, 'Peppermint.' He got me laughing. He was about the last one aboard."

The fingers of Kirkman's hand, flat on his desk, spread out slowly.

"Jesus," he said. "Think of all the people who are dead."

109

Fifteen

"It's not 'It's an honest ghost, let me tell you that.' It's 'It is an honest ghost, that let me tell you'!"

Everyone on the stage turned to the man who had exploded up from his aisle seat in the empty, dark theater.

"Furthermore, it's not 'I hold it fitting we shake hands and part.' It's 'I hold it fit that we shake hands and part'!"

"Look, Baird," one of the men on the stage, the director, said. He wore glasses and was holding an opened manuscript.

"And it's not 'What heart of man would think it?' It's 'Would heart of man once think it?'! Goddamn it!"

"Baird, will you let me do this my way?"

"No, fuck it, no!"

"Baird, listen to reason. You asked me to fly in from Chicago to work with Roddy."

"He isn't even getting the words right!"

"Jesus, Baird, what do you expect?" said Roddy, the Hamlet-to-be or not-to-be. "Last Sunday I was playing *The Music Man* in Miami."

"I don't give a Goddamn," Baird Hastings yelled from the dark. "You're not making him get the words right, Tony!"

"Let's get things blocked out first, Baird, okay? He

has to know where he is on the stage. This is a bigger stage than he's ever worked with before."

"You can say that again," muttered Hastings. "I want him onstage tonight!"

The director looked apologetically to the star before speaking reasonably to the producer. "That's not going to happen, Baird. You'll have to use the understudy again. Or close for a few days."

"I'm not going to use that mother-fucking understudy again! He was terrible last night. 'Get thee to a nunnery: why wouldst thou be a breeder of sinners.' *UGH!* Rod, you told me you played Hamlet last year. I know you did!"

"I did, Baird. In Toledo, Davenport, Butte. But that was last spring. Almost a year ago!"

"He has to get back into it, Baird," Tony said. "It will take a few days. You should close the show."

"I can't close the show. Closing it a few days means closing it forever! If you guys want to work, that curtain opens tonight. And that, that, that 'wretched, rash, intruding fool' hasn't even got the words right!"

The star muttered, "No, but I sure can sing 'Seventy-six Trombones.' "

"Give us a chance, will you, Baird? Go away and let us work."

"*Hamlet* wasn't written yesterday."

"Please, Baird. Let us work. We're doing the best we can."

When Baird Hastings marched out of the theater, the ghost of all Elsinore behind him, Flynn followed.

He followed him to the corner table in a small, dark bar-restaurant next door.

"Give me a double anything," Hastings snarled at the waiter. "Gin. Give me a martini."

"Will you be having lunch, Mister Hastings?"

"Fuck off," Hastings said. "Unless you can play Hamlet."

"Of course I can play Hamlet," the waiter said.

Flynn was standing in the darkness over Hastings' table.

"Good God." Hastings looked at him. "It's the King of Denmark. Come to haunt me."

"Actually, I'm Inspector Flynn. Come to question you. Regarding the death of Daryl Conover."

"Oh. You're the ghost of Daryl Conover."

"In a manner of speaking," said Flynn. "I am a spook."

With effort, Flynn fitted himself to the minute bar table and chair.

"What's to question? The son of a bitch died in an air crash. Served the bastard right. Blew him to bits. I'd have paid top dollar to see it. Have a drink? Do you happen to know the words to *Hamlet?*"

"No," drawled Flynn. "But I sure can sing 'Seventy-six Trombones.' "

Baird Hastings looked closely at Flynn across the gloom.

"Were you in the theater?" he asked. "That was funny, wasn't it? 'No, but I sure can sing "Seventy-six Trombones." ' When I'm trying to open him in *Hamlet!* Tonight! Jeez. I'm gonna cry!"

To laugh better, the two big men pushed the little vinyl-topped table away from both of them.

Still laughing, Flynn said, "So you blew up a hundred and eighteen people Monday night?"

"The next line is—" Roaring with laughter, Hastings put his hands under his tweed jacket onto his vest. "The next line is, 'So what did you do Tuesday'?"

"Actually, it was Tuesday morning. What are you doing today?"

"No, no. The next line is, I say, 'Tuesday I rested.' Is that funny?"

"It is, if you're near a nervous breakdown."

The waiter put the drink on the table and Hastings grabbed it, soberly.

"I'm near a nervous breakdown."

"Second one I've seen today," said Flynn. "Ah, well," he said, "anything for a laugh."

Quietly, firmly, Hastings said, "Monday we opened *Hamlet*. At the Colonial Theater. In Boston."

"And you and Conover had an argument."

"What did you say your name is?"

"Flynn. Inspector Flynn."

"The night a big production like this opens, everybody's uptight and exhausted at the same time. We've been through hell with each other—physically, intellectually, emotionally. Everybody hates everybody on opening night. Understand? That's why everybody's so phony—huggy and kissy. Understand?"

"Understood."

"Which is why nobody should be drinking. It makes the cauldron boil over."

"That's *Macbeth*," said Flynn. "Shouldn't mix semaphores."

"Which is why I blew my wig when I found Conover having an after-dinner drink in his dressing room, with friends. I just didn't expect it. Usually, you know, the really great British actors are better trained than that. It was his right, I guess. He's an old pro. I just didn't expect it. Of course, I was uptight."

"Understood."

"The first act went beautifully. My life's dream come true. Daryl Conover playing Hamlet in a Baird Hastings production. Really, he was wonderful. Between acts I tried to explain to him. You know, apologize.

113

I said there were kids, less professional actors, uptight kids, seeing him drinking before curtain. I told him how much his playing Hamlet meant to me. I made the mistake of telling him I had my own life's savings in the production."

"That was a mistake?"

"Right away he got suspicious. He thought I was running the show out of receipts."

"I don't understand that."

"It means the producer puts up whatever collateral he has to guarantee the craft unions' bonds. He pays for everything else out of loans and box-office receipts. He even pays off the interest on the loans out of box-office receipts. Get it?"

"No."

"It means that every dollar that comes into the box office immediately goes out the back door to keep the show running. The production isn't capitalized. Even salaries come out of the box office. Immediately."

"So?"

"Well, Inspector, this is the way a producer finances a new, off-Broadway play with one set and three characters. It's not the way you produce Daryl Conover playing Hamlet."

"He accused you of this?"

"Yes."

"Well?"

"He was right." Hastings swallowed the rest of his drink. "It's true."

"I see. You weren't properly financed to do what you were doing."

"I could have been. But I wasn't. Something crazy. I wanted to make this production entirely my own. So I made the producer's basic mistake. I provided no

114

financial backup. Of course, I was very sure of myself. And of Daryl Conover."

"And, I expect you had a certain confidence in Mister Shakespeare?"

"He blew his wig. Did he ever! He exploded! Why didn't he know this before? If he had, he would never have agreed. He'd been taken, raped, fucked. He couldn't pay British taxes as it was. He couldn't afford to work, he couldn't afford not to work; he certainly couldn't afford to come to America to work for nothing. I didn't think he was going back onstage for Act Two."

"But he did."

"He was magnificent. Daryl Conover was a real great actor. Bless his bits. However, Inspector, between the second and third acts he made a plane reservation for London."

"You knew it?"

"He left his door open while he made the phone call. He declaimed his reservation. All backstage was buzzing with it. I knew it."

Hastings waved at the waiter for a second drink.

"The third act was magnificent. Just magnificent. He had to stop the curtain calls. Backstage, I tried to reason with him, telling him he was ruining me, okay, but he was also ruining everyone else in the cast, everyone who had anything to do with the production. I told him opening night had gone so well we had nothing to worry about, financially or any other way. We'd move into New York in three weeks, on schedule. He reverted to himself, once off the stage. So angry his face was blue. He couldn't even speak. By actual count, he slammed three doors in my face."

"You couldn't keep him off the plane, so you blew the plane up, is that it?"

"I knew he was going on a plane, Inspector, but I didn't know which one."

"Easy enough to find out. Also, how many planes are there leaving for London from Boston at three o'clock in the morning?"

Hastings put his hand around his fresh drink.

"Funny. Until this moment I never thought of myself as a what-do-you-call-it, a defendant, possibly."

"As a prime suspect."

"Inspector, let me ask you this: How would I, Baird Hastings, blow up an airplane?"

"Let me answer you, Baird Hastings. First, your real name is Robert Cullen Hastings. That's the name under which you served in the United States Army. And, I hasten to remind you, the U.S. Army trained you as a demolition expert."

"Oh, my God."

" 'Oh, my Cocky' would be a better epithet, under the circumstances."

"You know I was trained as a demolition expert."

"I do. Drink up. There's more to come."

"Still, how could I blow up an airplane?"

"By jumping into your car as soon as all your arguments had failed against Conover, driving to your home in Beverly Farms, there picking up the dynamite you had bought to blow up a rock ledge on your property—"

"Oh, my God!"

"Oh, my Cocky. Manufacturing a bomb, driving it to Logan Airport—there was plenty of time, for all this —and rigging it aboard Flight 80 to London."

"Inspector, come on! Security at airports is a hell of a lot better than it used to be. You can't tell me—"

"I can tell you that somebody put a bomb aboard that airplane. And you can't tell me that Baird Hast-

116

ings, the theater producer, couldn't rig himself some kind of an innocent-looking airport workman's costume, and find his way out to the rear, right cargo hatch of that plane!"

"Jesus!"

"Cocky!"

"I'm not that cocky, Inspector. I wouldn't have the balls to carry off such a thing. Are you kidding? Kill a hundred people?"

"You were a ruined, devastated man, Robert Cullen Hastings. A man who grabbed himself up from nowhere into the magnificent tweed jacket of theater producer Baird Hastings, capping his career with a presentation of Daryl Conover playing Hamlet, and you blew it! Is that the right expression, or am I making a pun? You said yourself you were in a terrible state of nerves. You said yourself you'd pay top dollar to see Daryl Conover blown to bits. You did see him, Robert Hastings! You stood by a window at Logan Airport and watched!"

Hastings glanced around the bar-restaurant. For all its force, Flynn's voice had remained very low.

"You can't be serious, Inspector."

"You had the reason to do it. The man had ruined you."

"But not to kill a hundred other people."

"Ach, well, that! If you weren't of a dramatic temperament, you wouldn't be in the business you're in."

"Everyone associated with theater is crazy, right?"

"You're apt to think in the large."

"Inspector, you're talking about murder. Mass murder."

"Next, you had the material. Dynamite."

"I don't. I've used it."

117

"I thought you'd say that. And I'm sure no expert in the world, including yourself, can prove you've used all of it. Is that right? You could have had a stick or two in your old lunch pail."

Hastings' face was becoming clearer in the dim bar. He was growing white.

"Next, you have the education to use it."

"Inspector, that was twenty years ago. Twenty-five. I haven't used explosives in twenty-five years."

"You have enough confidence left in yourself to go out and buy the dynamite to blow up a ridge in your yard."

Hastings exhaled, deeply. "Right."

"You had the time, you had the opportunity. I do believe a theater producer could figure out how to give himself access to that plane."

Hastings said, "Are you arresting me?"

Flynn said, "Are you confessing?"

Hastings said, "I'm not confessing."

Flynn said, "I'm not arresting you."

Hastings, white-faced, slump-shouldered, looked up at Flynn standing in the gloom.

"Why not?" Hastings asked.

"There are one or two other leads to follow."

"But I am a prime suspect?"

"You're as prime as the beef the Australians themselves eat. All I wanted to know from this little exercise was whether you and Conover had a fight that night—if it was you Conover was furious with. It surely was."

Hastings' head lowered.

"May I say one thing, Inspector?"

"In your defense?"

Softly, to his drink, Baird Hastings said, "It was the best production of *Hamlet*—ever!"

118

Sixteen

It was a raw, cold morning in Dorchester, the east wind blowing in off the harbor a block away.

Flynn turned up his coat collar while waiting for someone to answer the door of the white, wooden, two-family duplex house.

"Mrs. Wiggers?"

Flynn touched the brim of his tweed hat to the middle-aged woman in an apron the other side of the glass storm door.

She opened it enough to hear him.

"I'm Inspector Flynn. The Boston Police. By any chance is your husband at home?"

"He's asleep," she said.

"He's at home?"

"Sleeping."

"I need to speak to him."

"Is it important?"

"It's about the airplane that exploded."

"All right." Flynn helped her open the door against the wind.

"It's not a pleasant day, Ma'am."

"It's a Boston day." Her arm suggested he turn to the left, into a small living room. "I'll wake him up."

The parlor was small, furnished with a two-seater divan, a pine coffee table, two easy chairs, a rug, a television, but as clean as a bride's linen. Jesus Christ was on one wall, pointing to his exposed heart, halo around his head; on the other wall was a framed print of a schooner in a rough sea. On the coffee table were copies of the *Catholic Digest*.

"A long-suffering woman," Flynn muttered to himself. "Her man's out at three in the morning and asleep at almost noon. Not a witness, I think, from whom I can expect much."

The step coming down the stairs was even.

The man turned into the living room.

"Richard Wiggers?"

"Yes."

Richard Wiggers was tall, broad-shouldered, slim, tight-skinned, and perfectly clear-eyed.

"I'm Inspector Flynn. How are you?"

"Sit down, Inspector."

"I will." Flynn did so. "I take it no one official has been to see you about your report that you saw a rocket hit the airplane yesterday morning?"

"Just the newspapers." Wiggers sat at complete ease in the other armchair. "That's rather surprised me."

"Everything in its time," said Flynn. "The FBI are still working on their initial report. Were you just asleep? You don't look it."

Wiggers needed a shave, but not badly.

"I'm used to waking up."

"Aren't we all, though?"

"I mean, and being ready to move out."

"Of course," said Flynn, gently. "Now, I guess my first question, however embarrassing it might be to you, is, what were you doing out at three o'clock yesterday morning? Having a bite at the old vine?"

"What?"

120

"Why were you out at three o'clock in the morning yesterday?"

"I'm out at three o'clock every morning."

"Oh, it's that way, is it?"

"Inspector, I drive an ambulance. In fact, I own an ambulance company. Wiggers Ambulance Service."

"You do?"

"Only three wagons, but it's mine."

"The Lord loves sardines. You weren't partying?"

"Partying? No. I don't drink and none of the men who work for me drink. Can't drink and drive, Inspector."

"I've heard it said."

"Actually, I was on a run from Boston City Hospital to our garage. I had just delivered a coronary."

"I see. And were you alone?"

"No. Ray was with me. Ray Tuborg. Another old fire buddy."

"I'm not with you."

"We all used to work for the Fire Department. Mostly the Rescue Squad. Dad left me this house, so even when our kids were little I was able to put money away. I bought an ambulance and moonlighted with it. It turned into a good business. So I quit altogether and bought a new ambulance. The first was secondhand. Then I bought another, and another."

"The American success story."

Wiggers shrugged. "I'm about where I would be if I had stayed in the Fire Department, except I own three ambulances, some equipment, and the garage over on Bernays Street. I just pay a different kind of taxes, is all. The reason I'm telling you all this," Wiggers said, "is because I'm puzzled."

"About what?"

121

"I was in the Fire Department eleven years. The Boston Fire Department."

"Yes?"

"You said you are Inspector Flynn. There are no inspectors in the Boston Police Department. There's no such rank."

"There's one," said Flynn. "Me."

"I don't get it."

"Well," said Flynn, "many don't. Truth is, the Commissioner gave me a special rank so if people said, 'The Inspector did this' or 'didn't do that,' he'd know just whom to blame."

"Oh."

"We were talking about the rocket. Would you care to describe it to me?"

"It was a rocket."

"Thank you."

"I mean, what else could it have been?"

"I didn't see it."

"It came out of the water just beyond the mouth of the harbor. It shot up."

"What color was it?"

"I didn't see it. I mean, in the moonlight it was silver like one of those pencils, only chopped off at the stub. Mostly what I saw was the flame behind it."

"Where were you when you saw it, Mister Wiggers?"

"Morrissey Boulevard. On the bridge, there, you know, by Malibu Beach."

"And you must have seen the rocket in the east, traveling west. Right?"

"Yes. Somewhat northwest."

"In other words, the rocket was coming more toward you than anything else?"

"No, it was going into the northern side of the harbor. I did not have the sensation it was coming straight at me."

"I'm just wondering how you saw the flame behind it."

"I didn't see the source of the flame, Inspector. I just saw the flame—what do you call it?—spurting out. The back."

"I see. And did this man Tuborg see it, too?"

"No. I said, 'Look at that!' Ray was half asleep. I braked there, on the bridge. In the moonlight, I saw the vapor trail of the jet, of the airplane. The rocket intersected with it. Actually, it looked as if it were going above and behind the airplane."

"And did the rocket leave a vapor trail?"

"No. I don't know. It went too fast. Instantly, the sky was lit up by the plane exploding. So I wouldn't have seen it. When Ray heard the explosion he sat up and said, 'What in hell is that?' "

"But he didn't see the rocket?"

"No."

"You mean, you said something to your partner, Ray Tuborg, about the rocket before the plane explosion? You said to him, 'Look at that'?"

"Yes."

"Before the plane exploded?"

"Yes."

"Will he verify that?"

"He has."

"Well," said Flynn, "I suppose I should ask you what you did next."

"We turned around, hit the siren, and headed for Logan Airport."

"Why did you do that?"

"I drive an ambulance, Inspector."

"Ah! Thick of me. But the explosion was over the harbor."

"I know. I guess it was just instinctive. We saw a

plane blow up, so we headed for the airport. In fact, we did make an ambulance run."

"From the airport?"

"A girl, you know, the girl who took the tickets for that flight—what do you call them, stewardesses?—went into extreme shock. She kept fainting. She kept saying, 'Daryl Conover, Daryl Conover.' "

"Probably the only passenger she recognized."

"We ran her to Mass. General. I think they put her under sedation. I don't know."

"Okay, Mister Wiggers." There was the sound of a vacuum cleaner operating upstairs. "The Civil Aeronautics Board told us this morning they have complete confidence in their evidence that the plane was blown up from inside. Inside a cargo hold."

Wiggers looked steadily, evenly at Flynn without saying anything.

Flynn said, "What do you say to that?"

"Nothing," Wiggers said evenly. "Inspector, I don't know about rockets, and I don't know about airplanes."

"You only know what you saw, is that it?"

"I only know what I think I saw. The mind can play funny tricks. There are people who insist they've seen flying saucers, too."

"Have you ever seen a flying saucer?"

"Nope."

"Tell me, Mister Wiggers, how did the newspapers get ahold of this story, that you'd seen a rocket?"

"At the airport. There were reporters there. We were all talking. I said the plane had been hit by a rocket. I thought other people had seen the rocket. And they all jumped on me."

"And the United States Navy had ships at sea within the hour."

"In the last—what's it been?—twenty-four, thirty-six hours I keep expecting someone else to say he saw the rocket."

"Do you feel foolish?"

"Well, you feel foolish when you're the only person in the world who saw something. I mean, I feel like one of these people who reports seeing flying saucers."

"I expect so."

Wiggers rubbed his whiskers and shrugged.

"I saw a rocket."

Seventeen

"Well, Cocky." Flynn settled down behind his desk. "So far today I've smoothed Grover's feathers, as much as he'd let me, visited a few pawnshops, examined bits and pieces of an airplane, interviewed a Zephyr Airways passenger representative, a Broadway producer, and a perfectly sober man who insists he saw a rocket rise up from the sea and hit a 707. At least we won't be bothered by Grover fetching us a gratuitous lunch today. I sent him home, hoping he'll get the idea of staying there for good and all."

Cocky handed Flynn an unopened telegram.

"What's this, now?" Flynn opened it. "Such shyness on your part? I expect you've had the message over the telephone anyway."

Cocky grinned.

"Ah, I see." Flynn read it: "MEET WITH FRINGS MATTOCK WINTON KASSEL WINTON THREE THIRTY BANK TODAY ROME COOL RAIN—NNO. You didn't understand the message, so you choose not to know about it. You're a shrewd, diplomatic man, Cocky."

Flynn was spared the silence of Cocky's not inquiring (and the silence of Flynn's not answering) by the ringing telephone.

"Frank?"

"Himself. Inspector Francis Xavier Flynn here, the Boston Police Department, Old Records Building, third floor, Craigie Lane, Boston, Massachusetts, New England, U.S. of A., deliveries at the rear, if you please. And who might you be?"

"Tim Reagan, Frank. Captain Reagan."

"Ah! For some reason I was expecting a Fibby named Hess."

"Frank, has anyone ever told you that some of the things you say don't make sense?"

"I think I've heard my wife mention that. Once or twice."

"I mean, you're brilliant, Frank, but—"

"I know the frustration, of trying to understand. My best advice to you is simply to sit back and let it roll over you."

"Sergeant Whelan is here. At headquarters."

"Old Grover? I thought he was spending the day quietly in his kennel."

"What happened to him, anyway, Frank? He's all beat up."

"What happened to him, did you ask?"

"He won't tell us. Black eye, cut cheek, swollen lips—"

"Ah, that! He mentioned, obliquely, mind you, something this morning about being attacked by a couple of violinists in Harvard Square last night."

"Violinists?"

"Yes. Now, who in his right mind would take on a couple of violinists, tell me that. But what's Grover doing at headquarters?"

"Trying to book someone for mass murder. For the airplane explosion the other night. I thought if you don't know what he's doing, or trying to do, you should."

"I ought. Whom is he trying to charge this morning?"

"Mrs. Charles Fleming."

"Sassie Fleming?"

"The Judge's wife."

"Grover arrested Sassie Fleming?"

"Handcuffs. The whole bit."

Flynn said, "Great! I'll be right over."

"You mean you are charging her?"

"No," said Flynn. "I'm taking her to lunch."

Eighteen

"Really, Inspector, if you wanted to have lunch with me, a simple invitation by telephone would have caused me to give the request full consideration. It was not necessary for you to send half the police force of the City of Boston and the Village of Kendall Green to bang down my door, frisk me, read me my rights in a loud and unintelligible shout, handcuff me, and whisk me, sirens blaring, into your jurisdiction. I'll have the escargots." Elbows on the white tablecloth, Sassie Fleming folded her hands primly in the air. She had handcuff marks on both wrists. "You might have more confidence in your personal sexual magnetism. Of course, you may have felt that to invite me to lunch within twenty-four hours of my learning of my widowhood would be improper, as, indeed, it would be. But surely it would not have been as unconscionable as this grievous aggression against my person, my privacy, and my mourning. And, I think, a green salad."

"Is that all?" asked Flynn.

"No," said Sassie. "A glass of the white table wine would be nice, too."

Flynn told the waiter their needs.

Sassie said, "Tell me you had nothing to do with having me arrested."

"I had nothing to do with having you arrested. I had

129

sent Grover to his kennel to lick his wounds on his straw pallet—which is what I thought he was doing."

"How did he get so beat up, anyway?"

"Oh, that. Grover has a spectacularly unsuccessful arrest record."

"I didn't mind him appearing at the door, writ in one hand and a bolt of lightning in the other, but Kendall Green being out of your jurisdiction, he had to be accompanied to my house by a Kendall Green policeman. There are only two. I found it all rather embarrassing. Especially after my efforts this last year to get a motion through the village council to get new uniforms for both of them."

"I can't apologize," Flynn said. "I didn't do it. I didn't know he was doing it. How are things otherwise?"

"I'm better than I might be. I borrowed somebody's horse yesterday afternoon, after you left, and had a lovely, long, hard ride by myself."

"Is that what you do to make yourself feel better?"

"One has to do something, Frank. One can't sit in a dark corner and cry to oneself. I'll go back to work next week. Monday. And then it will be spring, and I can get the garden going."

"How long were you married to the Judge?"

"About five years." They had been served, and they were eating. "Now you're going to give me a lot of dime psychoanalysis about my marrying someone old enough to be my father."

"I'm not."

"I have not suffered the lack of a father. My father is alive, well, working. We're very close. Charlie and I were real lovers. His being twenty-two years older than I necessarily took some of the edge off it, of course. I mean, we knew that I would be more sexually interested than he, as time went on, but we never thought I should

130

give up my sexual independence. Although I virtually did. Charlie was so exciting intellectually, and as a person, that—"

"Eat your snails. I didn't have you to lunch to grill you."

"You didn't?"

"No."

"Then why did you?"

"You should have more confidence in your sexual magnetism."

"Really?" Sassie's laugh was a little confused, a little embarrassed. "You're just trying to buck up an early widow."

"Maybe."

She said, "Inspector Francis Flynn. Married. Four children—"

"Five. Jeff is ten months old."

"In love with your wife."

"Deeply," said Flynn. "Totally."

He sat back from his omelette, holding his napkin in his lap.

"For all that," he said, "a man has a natural instinct, against any woman's compulsion to comprehend him totally, however indebted he may be to her, however loving he is of her, however fast friends they may be, against her thinking she knows all about him, can record every moment of his day and night, capture him, pin his wings against a board. He needs himself, some sense of himself beyond her, his own self. It's hard for a man, when he loves deeply and well. But for her sake, as well as his own, he is himself, and has a private self; he does love, and play, individually. No matter how close she is, he has to die alone. For this good reason, if for none other, no man, no woman, however much in love, ever gives up being alone. He never gives up individuality. He never gives up privacy. He lives, for the best of everyone. This must be true of woman, as well, God love us all."

Sassie looked at her plate a long time.

"At least your psychoanalysis is kindly," she said. "And I expect it's worth more than a dime."

"At least eleven cents," said Flynn.

"You're really very reassuring. In the right, odd way."

"I'll include it in a little book of sermonettes," Flynn said, "called *Yes, There Is a World Out There.*"

"Do," said Sassie. "Send me a copy."

"I might even hand-deliver." Flynn ordered tea for them both." I take it you haven't heard much from your stepson. Charles, Junior. Chicky, is he called?"

"Chicky. I haven't heard a word from him. Is there any way he couldn't know his father was killed?"

"Everyone in the world knows it."

"I guess he's been mourning in his hole, and I've been mourning in mine. I guess I should have called him."

"I guess he should have called you," said Flynn.

"Death in the family is no time to draw lines," Sassie said. "Be stand-offish."

"Then why haven't you called him?"

"I just— I don't know. I just haven't wanted to get into that whole Chicky-thing."

"Which is what?"

"Charlie's death is hard enough to take, without surrounding myself with Chicky immediately. Am I being selfish?"

"I don't know. What's wrong with Chicky?"

"He has his problems," she said. "He's a gambler. Compulsive. Gets into these gambling fevers. Nothing can stop him. God knows we've tried. Married young. She walked out on him, of course. Thank God there were no children. Chicky couldn't keep in possession of anything. I mean, truly. He sold the toaster. He sold the bed."

"He's a pharmacist?"

"Yes. And he's almost always kept a job. Although how, I don't know. He gets into these gambling fevers and he's not rational. He's not sane. I would think he'd be dangerous, you know, making up a prescription for somebody when he's on one of these crazy streaks. He insists he's never more sane. He hasn't killed anybody yet—as far as we know."

"Surely you and the Judge would have gotten him to a psychiatrist by now."

"Dozens of them. It doesn't take. He resists the whole thing. I think basically he resists me, as much of the work I do is in criminal psychology. So he resists any shrink we send him to. Every time Chicky's come a cropper and Charlie's had to pay his way out of it, the deal has been that in return Chicky would get himself to a psychiatrist and work hard at getting himself cured. Never works."

"What have his debts amounted to?"

"Oh, three thousand dollars. Seven thousand dollars a year ago. Twelve thousand dollars six months ago. Nice the way these bastards keeping extending his credit, isn't it?"

"He hasn't asked for anything in the last six months?"

Sassie said, "Not as far as I know."

"You do know," said Flynn. "You know that that walk Chicky and the Judge took in the woods on Sunday was another request for money."

"I don't absolutely know it," said Sassie.

"You don't know it, but you think so."

"Yes. I think so."

"You said the Judge was a little depressed when he came back from the walk."

"He was. But he didn't tell me what it was about."

"Did he usually tell you about Chicky's debts?"

"Sooner or later."

"But he didn't this time."

"He was leaving for England the next night. He probably didn't want to throw something sad and ugly at me at that point."

"You say the Judge didn't have any real money?"

"No. He didn't. Our incomes ran ahead of our expenses, so we had savings accounts, of course. We'd put money in savings and sooner or later Chicky would need it. This last amount, the twelve thousand dollars —Charlie had to borrow half of it from the bank."

"Is it all paid back?"

"Yes. I'm pretty sure it is. I don't think there's much in savings, though." Sassie pushed the empty teacup away from her. "Poor Chicky. So mixed up. His father was so important, so bright, so beautiful. There was no way for Chicky to compete decently. Away down deep, I think Chicky thought too well of his father—to his own detriment. He worshiped him. Charlie was God. I don't know whether this whole gambling compulsion was Chicky's way of punishing his father or himself. It worked both ways. Either he's been trying to prove his father wasn't God, or that he was. I can't imagine what he'll do now."

"Sassie," Flynn said. "There's something you have to face. There's a real possibility your husband needed a lot of money when he got on that plane to England the other night."

"I realize that, Frank." But her eyes were hurt. "I'm not telling you anything I haven't worked out for myself. But it doesn't work that way."

"What doesn't?"

"I got a letter this morning. You remember either

134

Grover or you said I'd get the half-a-million dollars' worth of insurance policies in this morning's mail?"

"Yes," said Flynn. "Actually, I said it."

"Well, I didn't. They're smarter than that. This morning I got a letter in the mail instead telling me there's a limit of one hundred and twenty-five thousand dollars on flight insurance. Apparently there was a big sign right there, saying so. We were tiddily. People were shoving by us. If we were thinking of the insurance as insurance, instead of some silly game we were playing, we would have noticed that sign, don't you think?"

"I don't know. Frankly," said Flynn, "I find the contention that someone would not murder himself and one hundred and seventeen other people for one hundred and twenty-five thousand dollars, but would do so for five hundred thousand dollars, more than a little capricious. Sign or no sign."

"And anyway," Sassie said, "the letter went on to say even the one hundred and twenty-five thousand dollars will not be paid until the satisfactory conclusion of an investigation."

"I see."

"So it means nothing, Frank. Nothing."

"It means nothing now."

"What do you mean?"

"It might have meant something to the Judge on Monday."

"He was a careful man, Inspector. He wouldn't make such a mistake, if it were significant."

"On the other hand, Mrs. Fleming, one might expect a federal judge to consider himself and his wife above suspicion, in most matters. Most crimes require some conceit. Well, now." Flynn was paying the check. "I shouldn't worry you about this anymore, in your grief."

"Thank you."

"I said at the beginning of lunch I wasn't grilling you."

"You did."

"Then this matter about Chicky came up."

"One of us brought it up."

"Was it myself, by any chance?"

"I think it was, Inspector."

"Well, once on the table it needed a chew. I believe it best if you're prepared for all contingencies. Even if it's only a matter of having to confront your stepson —which you will have to do one day, you know."

"I know."

"By the way, if Chicky is in debt again, will you take it upon yourself to pay his debts?"

"I suppose so."

"Forever?"

"No," Sassie said. "This would be the last time."

"Are you sure of that, now?"

"Absolutely sure."

"I hope so. Come on, I'll find you a taxi."

"Do I dare leave your presence?"

"What do you mean?"

"Grover. Your Sergeant Richard T. Whelan. How do I know he's not lurking outside the door, ready to snap at me with handcuffs again?"

"Since he insisted upon working the day, I sent him out to interview the widow of the other deceased who had the prescience to insure his last gasp—however, for only five thousand dollars. Burial expenses, I'd say: a modest man. A woman named Geiger, in Newton."

"I feel sorry for her, whoever she is."

"Have no fear," Flynn said. "Nobody will arrest you henceforth, except, possibly, myself."

Nineteen

"Come in, Mister Flynn." The man in the dark brown suit stood up behind a mammoth desk.

It was just three-thirty.

Two other men in side chairs rose to shake hands as well.

"I'm Henry Winton. This is Clarke Frings and Robert Mattock."

Flynn shook hands all around. He had been relieved of his overcoat downstairs.

On one wall of the office was a Turner seascape.

"Well," Winton said. "Did you have a nice flight from Rome?"

"Very nice," said Flynn.

"Rome is lovely this time of year."

"It was raining when I left," said Flynn. "Cool."

He had wondered why N. N. had telegraphed him the Rome weather report. Anything to keep Flynn's cover straight.

As he had not been telegraphed what organization he was supposedly representing, he was reasonably sure the question would not arise.

His credibility had been established efficiently by his knowing what the weather had been that morning in Rome.

"Sit down, Mister Flynn. We'll answer any questions to the best of our ability."

The Kassel-Winton Bank had not been easy to find.

Down an alley in the old Huguenot section of Boston, Bay Village, the bank was far from the city's financial center. Looking at the alley from across the street, one could only see a coffee shop.

To enter the alley, Flynn had to mount three of the stone-apron stairs leading to the coffee shop, and walk down their other side.

Number 11 (there were only six addresses in the alley) was the middle building, on the left. The far end of the alley was blocked by stout posts and a chain.

He had to ring a doorbell and wait until a small man opened a small door to him. Flynn identified himself by name only. The small man seemed mostly interested in seeing that Flynn was alone; that no one else lurked in the alley.

After hanging Flynn's overcoat carefully in a hall closet, the man led Flynn up a carpeted flight of stairs.

On the lower floor, to his left, Flynn had seen a white-jacketed man clearing silver from a dining table. Two side doors in the dining room were open, to rooms beyond.

The upper storey, too, was extended well beyond the original size of the house, carpeted corridors going past several closed doors.

The Kassel-Winton Bank obviously was all three houses this side of the alley, with a single entrance.

The office to which he had been shown, Henry Winton's, enjoyed the central position in the three houses.

The four men sat in the comfortable room.

"Rashin al Khatid," Flynn said, removing his pipe from his breast pocket. "The Ifadi Minister of the Exchequer. I need to know everything."

"Yes," Clarke Frings said.

Robert Mattock said, "Mister Flynn, you understand, of course, that we never discuss our clients, or our clients' business. Mister Winton thinks there's reason in this instance for an exception to be made."

"There is." Flynn sucked on his cold pipe.

"I see," said Mattock.

"Mister Flynn," asked Frings, "is it conceivably true that Flight 80 to London the other morning was shot down by a rocket?"

"It is." Flynn continued to suck on his cold pipe.

"I think," said Winton, "we have every reason to answer Mister Flynn's questions."

"Yes," said Frings.

"First, Mister Flynn," proceeded Robert Mattock, "do you know that the Minister, his secretary, and bodyguard were in this country using United States passports especially prepared for them by the United States State Department?"

"I do." Flynn reached for his tobacco pouch in his jacket pocket.

"Names of Carson, Bartlett, and Abbott," said Frings.

"What were they doing here?" asked Flynn.

"A banking matter." Frings looked cautiously at Winton.

"Having to do with International Credits," said Winton.

"All very complicated," said Mattock.

"I daresay." Flynn tapped tobacco into the bowl of his pipe. "Perhaps you could explain."

Mattock and Frings looked at Winton.

"Well," said Winton. "You see," he said. He sat back in his chair in a studiously relaxed pose. "Our understanding is the new Republic of Ifad needs to replenish its arsenal."

"Ifad is buying weapons," said Flynn.

"Purely defensive weapons," said Mattock.

"From the United States," added Frings. "Which explains the United States passports, of course."

"How much?" asked Flynn.

"Well." Winton jerked forward in his chair. "That all depends on the value of money, of course, at any given time."

"How much," Flynn asked, "was the total arranged for in International Credits for the Republic of Ifad?"

Everyone, including Flynn, looked at Winton.

He said, "A quarter of a billion dollars."

Frings cleared his throat. "That really isn't much, Mister Flynn, when you consider what the level of international arms flow is at the moment."

Flynn said, "I know."

"This matter isn't as complicated as Mister Mattock indicated," said Winton. "You see, Ifad has a quarter of a billion dollars' worth of gold, built up over the last few years from their oil resources—"

"Where is the gold?" asked Flynn.

"In Ifad," said Frings, "buried in the courtyard of the presidential palace."

Flynn hesitated before lighting his pipe. "Are you serious?"

"I saw it two weeks ago."

"Literally," Flynn asked, "you mean it is buried in the President's backyard?"

"There are steps going down." Frings tried to show with his hands. "An iron door. Guards."

Winton laughed. "Exactly, Mister Flynn. You see, we, as bankers, have the responsibility of getting that money out of there, recycling it, as it were, putting it to work again, providing jobs—"

"—and guns for Ifad," added Flynn.

"Well, we'd provide anything," said Winton, "as long

as the money comes into our factories. What they want are guns."

"Guns are what they all want," said Mattock.

"What they should want," said Frings, "are air conditioners. Have you ever been to that part of the world, Mister Flynn?"

Flynn didn't answer.

"We talk to them about air conditioners," Winton said, "building food-freezing plants, irrigation systems—"

"What they want—" said Mattock.

"Are guns," said Frings.

"Right," said Flynn. "So you did arrange a quarter of a billion dollars in International Credits for the new Republic of Ifad?"

"Yes," Winton said.

"With which credits, Ifad is to buy a quarter of a billion dollars of American weapons?"

"Yes," said Winton.

"How does this work?" asked Flynn. "I'm particularly interested in the timing of it."

"Well—" Frings looked at Winton.

"I'm not sure I understand the question," said Mattock.

Flynn said, "The man got on the airplane at three o'clock in the morning and ten minutes later the plane blew up. I want to know what happened before that."

"I see," said Mattock.

"The Minister," Winton began, "Rashin al Khatid, arrived last week. Wednesday, was it?"

"Wednesday," confirmed Mattock.

"Of course, we knew about the proposition before he arrived. Clarke Frings had already been to Ifad for preliminary discussions—"

"To make sure they had the gold," said Frings.

Winton laughed. "That's right. Arrangements for such a matter as this are rather easy. Of course, we had the weekend in the way. By Monday night, late Monday night, we had already communicated with London, Zurich, Rome, and had had our final communication from Tokyo. We gave a little dinner downstairs for the Minister, signed the necessary remaining papers. What else happened? The Minister communicated with his capital. Mister Frings went in the car with them to the airport."

"He communicated with his capital, you said?" asked Flynn.

"Didn't he?" Winton asked Mattock.

"Actually, his secretary did. He sent the actual message."

"And what happened to the papers which were signed?"

"We're not prepared to expose those in detail, Mister Flynn," Winton said quickly. "I'm afraid you'd have to bring the full force of the law—I mean, United States law—to see them. Nothing under the rug, of course, but international credit communications, you know—I mean, we have our own international credit to consider."

"I didn't ask to see them," said Flynn. "I asked, what happened to them?"

"We have our copies," Winton said simply. "The Minister had his."

"He took them with him?"

"Yes," said Winton. "As far as we know. That would be normal procedure."

"We went forward with our communications of confirmation the next morning precisely as arranged," Mattock said. "Needless to say."

Flynn blinked at him. "Needless to say."

142

"Banking does go on," Winton said. "The death of a single man . . . I mean, these arrangements are so delicate."

"Tell me," Flynn said, as he resettled the contents of his pipe bowl. "About the Minister. What sort of a man was he?"

"Very cautious," said Mattock.

The three men laughed.

"I believe Mister Frings knew the Minister best," said Winton.

"We're laughing, Mister Flynn, because the Minister was, well, overly cautious."

"Even by our standards," said Mattock.

"A great deal of what we did between Wednesday and Monday," said Winton, "was, frankly, hand holding. This man, the Minister, had never been through this sort of a deal before. Well, what could you expect? He's only been in office a short time; it's a new government in Ifad—"

"Not a classy fellow?" asked Flynn.

"Well—" continued Winton, settling his dark green tie inside his dark brown suit, "they're a government newly in office; they find a quarter of a billion dollars in their basement, in gold; supposedly they're representing The People, doing their first deal with us big guys—"

"He was nervous?" asked Flynn.

"Scrupulous," said Frings.

"Overly cautious," repeated Mattock.

"He went over and over and over everything," said Frings. "He balked at the most common, standard phrases. Everything had to be translated seven ways to Sunday, and then reinterpreted and explained again and again."

"He didn't know what he was doing?" said Flynn.

143

"He didn't know what he was doing," agreed Winton. "Actually, Mister Flynn, there was no reason for his being here at all. We were glad to entertain him, of course, however difficult that was—"

The three men laughed again.

"—but really what we were doing was educating him on how to press buttons, you see. . . ."

"Why was entertaining him difficult?" asked Flynn.

"Oof! He was scrupulous that way, too," said Frings. "Food and drink. Impossible! Thursday morning we had to go out and hire an expert. A consultant. On how to entertain this fellow. No liquor, of course. Dietary laws I still don't understand. To the point of superstition."

"Usually, Mister Flynn," Winton explained, "Arabian businessmen these days are a little more flexible, in their personal habits. At least those sent abroad are."

"Even the Minister's secretary, Mihson, was somewhat flexible. Not Rashin. Even Mihson expressed a degree of exasperation."

"The Minister," said Winton, "was a very precise, deliberate, inflexible man."

"You were glad to see the back of him," said Flynn.

Winton smiled. "We would never say such a thing."

"And Mister Frings," asked Flynn, "you took him to the airport?"

"Yes," said Frings. "In the bank's Lincoln. Which then dropped me at my apartment."

"You didn't enter the airport with the Minister?"

"No," said Frings. "Didn't want to cause too much attention, you know. Bad enough as it was, the man traveling with a secretary and a bodyguard. Anyhow—"

"You were glad to see the back of him."

144

"I'd never say such a thing," said Frings.

"How did he act on the way to the airport? Normal?"

"For him. He sat in the corner of the back seat clutching his attaché case. Thanking us. For a nice time."

"Well," Flynn banged his pipe ashes into a gold ashtray on the desk. "So do I. Thank you. For a nice time."

Winton laughed. "You were no trouble, Mister Flynn."

Flynn said, "Are you sure of that, now?"

"Going back to Rome right away?" asked Mattock.

"Possibly."

Sincerely, Frings said, "I could take you to the airport, Mister Flynn."

"You could not," said Flynn. "You never know. I might be superstitious myself."

Twenty

If Sassie was right, that Charles Fleming's, Junior's, room on Forster Street was a complete mess, Flynn was never to know it.

Through the thin door, he heard two sports programs blaring simultaneously from radios.

Flynn had to pound his fist.

"Who is it?"

The radios did not diminish in volume.

"Inspector Flynn! Boston Police!"

"Go away!"

" 'Go away,' he says," muttered Flynn. "What kind of an imposter do I have to be to do my job now?" He shouted, "Open up! I need to talk with you!"

"You want to talk to me about my father!" Chicky's voice was near hysteria.

"I do! You're right, lad!"

Chicky's voice, quieter, much closer to the door, said, "Do you have a warrant?"

Flynn hesitated. The young man was the son of a judge. He probably knew what he was talking about. Cautiously, Flynn said, "What kind of a warrant?"

"A search warrant," Chicky said. "An arrest warrant."

Flynn said, "I've got a beguiling smile."

"Get out of here!" the voice shrieked.

"Listen, lad, I only need to talk with you. Not search you or arrest you!"

The volumes of both radios increased to crashing noise levels.

"Get the fuck out of here!" the voice shrieked, now fully hysterical. "Go away! Go away! Go away!"

"Ach, well." Flynn buttoned his overcoat. "There's a lad in more trouble than he knows ... standing on his rights."

Twenty-one

"Good-bye, Fucker."

Marion "Forker" (as the newspapers were obliged to write his name) Henry, ex-World Middleweight Champion boxer, had said nothing.

Flynn had questioned him gently, fairly sure the boxer was not a great repository of information, anyway.

The boxer, dejected, depressed, possibly recently catatonic, had remained sitting in the plastic chair in a bedroom of the suite in the cheap hotel near Boston Garden. The window shades were down. One bedside light shone dully. His shoulders extended far beyond the shoulder seams of his shirt; his arms far below the bottoms of his sleeves. The shirt was taut across his chest and voluminous around his waist. Clothes looked as inappropriate on Marion Henry as they would on a Greek statue, a Mack truck, or any other massive sculptural achievement.

Staring into the darkest corner of the room, Fucker had listened to Flynn's first questions without responding at all.

Finally, he put his mammoth hand to the crown of his head and wiped down his hair to his forehead a few times as if whisking off water after a shower, then rubbed his face, vigorously, in a circular motion. He sat forward, and put his hands on his chin.

He began to say something, and stopped.

The boxer was crying.

"Listen." Alf Walbridge closed the door between himself and Flynn in the living room and Fucker in the bedroom. "Inspector."

Alf Walbridge, Fucker's manager, was a skinny little man in a Stewart plaid vest.

"You got to understand."

"What do I have to understand?" asked Flynn.

"The kid's not himself."

"Who is he, then?"

"I haven't let any reporters see him at all. We should have been back in Detroit by now. The kid won't move." Alf jerked his thumb toward the bedroom door. "Percy Leeper's biggest mourner."

"I'm not sure I understand," said Flynn.

"Listen. Have you ever boxed?"

"Not by prearrangement," said Flynn.

"You look like you could've. Listen. You've got to get psyched up for it. Weeks you train. *I'm gonna kill the son of a bitch. I'm gonna kill the bastard.* Running five miles, working the bag, skipping rope, working with a partner—everything's done to the rhythm, *I'm gonna kill him, I'm gonna kill him.* Everybody says to you, *Kill the bastard, Fucker, kill him, kill him.*"

"I agree," said Flynn. "The metaphor is excessive."

"Listen. Think how he feels. He goes into the ring, ready to kill the bastard. It's a fair fight. He loses to the Leeper. He comes back, hurting bad, inside and out, really suffering, no press, suddenly he's a bum, and then he begins to really resent and hate. Got it? The psyching machinery we've been working on for weeks goes haywire. It always does. Then he really

149

wants to kill the bastard. They always talk rematch, right away, quick. They want it the next night. *I'll kill the bastard, Alf, I'll really kill him.* Then, while he's in this mood, three, four o'clock in the morning, whatever it was, he hears the fuckin' plane blew up, Percy Leeper's on it, blown all over the fuckin' harbor. Get it?"

"I think so," said Flynn.

"Listen, that kid in there is really suffering. He's got guilt for killing a hundred people. He believes he was really wishing the Leeper dead. It's very big in his mind. Can you understand?"

"I can understand," said Flynn. "But the thought never entered my wee mind that Fucker might be the assassin. I was thinking more of the people behind him, his friends and supporters."

Alf's chin jerked up. "What d'ya mean?"

"People like you. And your friends."

"What are ya talking about?"

"I'm talking about the mob," said Flynn.

"What are ya talking about? The mob."

"The mob," said Flynn.

"Jesus! Every time anybody says anything about the fight game, they're talking about the mob right away. Sure there's been money behind Fucker, invested in him, we aren't sure exactly where it all came from. There is in the real estate business, too. In the banking business. In the cookie business. In the police business, Flynn!"

"I expect you're right."

"So what are ya saying?"

"Supposing Percy Leeper had been paid to throw the fight and he found himself winning against your Fucker and decided he liked it, or maybe couldn't help himself and won anyway—"

"Never happened!" The little man was outsized by his own indignation. "Never happened!"

"What did happen," Flynn continued in his quiet voice, "is that Percy Leeper, after fighting a whole match, got on the first plane leaving this country— four hours later—and that plane blew up!"

"Never happened!"

"It happened," said Flynn. "The plane blew up."

"Listen. Leeper wanted to get home fast, while the fans were still cheering. Big airport scene. It always happens. It's good for endorsements."

"The plane blew up."

"Nothing like that happened. Listen. Are you crazy? The big guys don't play like that. Listen, how much would the payoff on a match like this be? A half a million? Maybe. A million? Not for the Middleweight. So you think the big guys would kill a hundred people because they lost a half a million bucks on a match? Don't be crazy."

"I don't know 'the big guys.' "

"A little guy? Maybe. Like this pharmacist here in town, in trouble a hundred grand, his banker, his uncle or somebody says no, credit's always been good, he's always paid, so he bets another hundred G's on Fucker. And loses."

"A pharmacist?"

"Now there's a desperate man. What d'ya say? A madman!"

"Was the pharmacist's name Fleming, by any chance?"

"I don't know. Heard about it in the bar downstairs. Chicky, Chicky something. He'd blow up an airplane. Killing a hundred people? The big guys are too cool for that, Flynn. And what d'ya think? You think only America's got a mob? Why don't you suspect the English mob paid us off to lose?"

"Did they?"

"No. Nobody paid anybody. This was a clean fight. When you get into a world championship match, Flynn, there's no funny stuff. Believe me. It gets too expensive. Too many eyes and ears. It would ruin the game. Listen." Alf picked up a newspaper off the coffee table and slapped it down again. "I admit. Fucker's beaten some fighters who are classier than he is. Okay? He got the championship fair and square. There's no way he could beat the Leeper. Everybody knew that except one stupid pharmacist in Boston. You think the big guys didn't know that? You're crazy. Maybe the whole thing was a setup. From the beginning. You get me? I admit. Somebody's been making that kid in there look better than he is. For a long time now. Leeper outclassed him. Outfought him."

The little man fell into a cheap, upholstered chair.

"With Leeper dead," asked Flynn, "who gets the World Championship now?"

"No one. It has to be contended."

"But Leeper's death puts your boy, Fucker, back at the top of the heap, doesn't it?"

"I suppose so."

"Even without the championship, he returns to his former position: he's the man to beat, right?"

Alf said, "I suppose so."

"You 'suppose so'? You know so. Otherwise you wouldn't be sitting here in this dank hotel room in Boston nursing the boyo. Would you?"

Alf Walbridge put his hands on top of his head and looked at Flynn.

"You know, Flynn. You're a brave man."

"It's possible," said Flynn, "that someone, or some

people did not want the Middleweight World Championship crown to leave the United States. When you consider all the possibilities resulting from control of the championship, you find yourself thinking of millions and millions of dollars, not just a few hundred thousand."

"You're on the wrong track, Flynn. Listen to me: absolutely the wrong track."

"Am I, indeed?"

"Absolutely on the wrong track." The man sat forward in his chair. He was sweating. "And if you're not," he said, quietly, "believe me, Fucker and I know nothing about it."

"I'm sure," said Flynn. "But I'm not sure that boyo sitting alone in that dark bedroom, doubled over with suffering, isn't giving the question full consideration, in at least one part of his damaged brain."

"I tell ya, his guilt is pure psychological."

"Call me," Flynn said, "if either one of you want to give me some names."

"Yeah, yeah," Alf Walbridge said. "We'll be in touch."

Twenty-two

"Not very well," Flynn answered into the telephone mouthpiece. "We've developed some interesting local leads, but we haven't had anything I'd call a real break yet."

At the other end of the line, John Roy Priddy— N. N. Zero—said nothing, waiting for Flynn to amplify.

Alone in his office, Flynn swiveled his desk chair, put his feet on the radiator, and looked out his window at the lights on the harbor.

"For example," he said, "the English actor, Daryl Conover, walked off an expensive production of *Hamlet* opening night, leaving the producer, Baird Hastings, with a bagful of cats meowing for their suppers. As Robert Cullen Hastings, our boyo was trained by the United States Army as a demolition expert. We also know he bought a quantity of dynamite to help in his gardening a short while ago."

"Sounds good," N. N. Zero said.

"Doesn't it, though? We know he didn't buy the dynamite to blow up the airplane—nothing that premeditated—but we know he could have had dynamite Monday night when Conover walked off on him, absolutely ruining him. And, after watching him a bit, I'd say he's a man of moods."

"Worth further investigation," N. N. Zero said.

"Yes. We would need to pin down precisely where Hastings was from eleven-thirty to three Monday night, Tuesday morning. Simple matter."

"You haven't done so?"

"Then," said Flynn, "there's the Human Surplus League joyfully claiming credit for the human fireworks display. Nobody seems to be getting anywhere at the job of finding them. As I told you, I sent my own lads, Todd and Randy, out to track them down. Haven't heard anything from them yet."

"Yes."

"There's another small possibility," Flynn said. "As I told you, aboard that plane was the English boxer, Percy Leeper. He had just won the World Middleweight Championship."

"What could he possibly have to do with it?"

"I'll tell you," Flynn said. "There's a rumor around that his opponent, Fucker Henry, the ex-champion, enjoyed pretty strong backing from the mob. Either they might have been double-crossed by Leeper, who couldn't help himself winning, despite after possibly being paid off. Or they simply didn't want to lose control of the Middleweight crown this side of the Atlantic. In either case, I understand, from only one source, mind you, that Leeper's timely demise makes Fucker Henry the top contender again—the man to beat. I would guess there could be millions involved in having control of the next championship matches, to say nothing of the illicit profits to be reaped from the resultant wagering."

" 'Fucker'? Is that what that nickname really is?"

"It is," said Flynn.

"The newspapers print it 'Forker.' "

"I know."

"Some smart guy I am. I never caught on."

"Newspapers still don't print the absolute truth of everything," said Flynn. "There's still some decency left."

"I always wondered what 'Forker' meant."

"It means 'Fucker,' " Flynn said gently.

"What else, Frank? Quit forking around."

"A man named Nathan Baumberg," Flynn said. "Vice-president of Zephyr Airways. In charge of aircraft maintenance. Either is or was involved with the Jewish Defense League."

"Phew."

"Precisely. However, I can't quite put this together. He had the motive, the opportunity, and, of course, the wherewithal. However, we have not developed evidence yet that Baumberg knew, or could have known, that Rashin al Khatid, the Ifadi Minister of the Exchequer, was aboard that plane, traveling under another name, on a U.S. passport, buying a quarter of a billion dollars' worth of arms for the Republic of Ifad."

"JDL Intelligence isn't that good, Frank."

"I wouldn't think so."

"Furthermore, the JDL would never do a thing like that. Kill over a hundred innocent people—"

"I wouldn't think so," said Flynn. "I'm sure not. But any fringe section of its members, or ex-members might. Trouble with a group like that, they can't always control their members. Especially their ex-members. People who left the JDL with one discontent or another."

"What would their purpose be in blowing up the plane—punitive?"

"Is there any way," Flynn asked, "they could stop the sale of arms by murdering Rashin al Khatid on his way home with a quarter of a billion in his pocket?"

"Funny you should say that, Frank. One of the two

things I have to tell you is that the sale of arms to the Republic of Ifad was canceled today."

"It was?"

"It was."

"All of it?"

"The whole quarter of a billion."

"Who canceled it? The United States?"

"No. The Republic of Ifad. No reason given. The United States was expecting to go through with the deal."

"There's no way anyone could have expected otherwise," Flynn said.

"I wouldn't think so."

"So maybe they were scared off."

"Maybe they were."

"Tell me, sir, has there been any announcement from Ifad concerning the death of their Minister of the Exchequer?"

"Not yet."

"Odd."

"Not so odd. The guy was traveling on a phony passport. Don't worry. He'll die next week in an auto accident in the Zol Desert."

"Then," said Flynn, "there's another intriguing lead. It has to do with a son who is a compulsive gambler. Always before his father's paid his debts for him. Now the lad is impossibly in debt. Daddy can't pay. He goes on that airplane, insured for half a million dollars— he thinks, or somebody thinks—and the airplane blows up."

"Name?"

"Fleming."

"Judge Fleming?"

"And son. A very sick young man. A very desperate young man."

157

"Sounds good."

"You said that before," said Flynn. "Two things wrong with it. So far, we haven't placed the son at the airport. As far as we know, he did not go to see his father off. And young Fleming isn't talking, voluntarily. Second, the son isn't the beneficiary of the insurance— his stepmother is.

"And then," Flynn continued, "we've got one hundred and twelve other people aboard that airplane. The above are just the immediately obvious leads."

"You've done well in a couple of days, Frank."

"We haven't even begun," Frank said. "As I said, we haven't had any real significant break yet. I haven't heard that bell ring, you know. Soon now, I'll give these leads to the FBI, all done up lovely in a package, with a ribbon, for them to follow up, and then I'll go see what else I can find."

"Don't despair, Francis."

"Wouldn't think of it. But trying to find the reason for the simultaneous deaths of one hundred and eighteen people . . . it's like *The Bridge of San Luis Rey,* if you take my meaning. There's a single cause, there has to be, but I wonder about so much more."

"Don't turn mystical, either."

"I'll suppress it. You said you had two things to tell me. What is the other?"

"The United States Navy has reported there was a Russian submarine in Massachusetts Bay, Monday night."

"You don't say! The idea of the rocket rears up again."

"They pursued. The decision not to apprehend the sub was made at the very highest level of United States government."

"Well, now, there's nothing mystical about that!"

158

"But, Frank, no one can figure out why the Russians would do such a thing—blow up an American commercial jet."

"To demonstrate to the world they can?"

"I think everybody knows they can, Frank."

"Do you suppose the wee Republic of Ifad is making war-like gestures at the mighty Union of Soviet Socialist Republics?"

John Roy Priddy laughed.

"Well," said Flynn, "could it have anything to do with the arms sale going to the United States?"

"Nonsense," said N. N. Zero. "We're only talking about a quarter of a billion dollars."

"Pardon my manners," said Flynn.

"Everybody's bigger than that."

"Still and all, as an example?"

"Would you believe it?"

"No."

"Thought not. Neither would I. You and I both have too much experience that side of the fence. Anything you need, Frank?"

"Yes. I want photos of Rashin al Khatid, Mihson Taha, and Nazim Salem Zoyad. Copies of their passport photos will do."

"I doubt it. As you realize, they were purposely made a little blurry."

"Better than nothing," said Flynn. "I want to discover what else our boyos did, other than penny-banking, while in Boston."

"They'll be on your desk in the morning."

"Thank you."

Cocky said, "Grover's waiting downstairs, in the car, to take you to the airport."

159

"And to the pawnshops," said Flynn. "Don't forget the pawnshops, on the way home."

Into the telephone, Cocky said, "Inspector Flynn's office."

"Ah, Cocky. A lovely, warm cup of Eyebright tea, well-steeped. Good in the gizzard."

Cocky handed Flynn the phone. "Hess. FBI."

"This is the President of the United States," Flynn said into the phone.

"Flynn," Hess said, "is it true you arrested Mrs. Charles Fleming this morning?"

"Yes," said Flynn. "It is."

"You went ahead and did a stupid thing like that, without even informing us?"

"I did," said Flynn.

"What in Christ's name made you do a thing like that?"

"I was inspired," said Flynn. "By staff."

"You mother-fucking, cock-sucking son of a bitch!"

"Now, now," said Flynn, "you're raising your voice."

"Son of a bitch!"

"Mind your manners," said Flynn, "or I'll have to put down the receiver and complain about an obscene phone call."

"I told you you're not to do anything without us!"

"I heard you."

"Then what the fuck do you mean by going out and arresting the wife of a federal judge for mass murder without a shred of evidence?"

Flynn tugged the ruby and diamond pin from his vest pocket—the pin I. M. Fletcher had sent Jenny—and looked at it, turning it this way and that in the light.

"It's all right," said Flynn. "I let the lady go, after giving her a nice French lunch."

160

"Jesus Christ!"

"The issue is over," said Flynn. "For the time being."

"It is like hell! For the last time, Flynn, I'm ordering you to report to the Command Center at the airport, at once!"

" 'Command Center'? Which do you call that, the broiling conference room, or the freezing hangar?"

"Get over here! Conference room! Now!"

"I wouldn't go near that airport," said Flynn, "if you were offering free ice cream to everyone under the age of forty-two!"

Twenty-three

"Airport," Flynn said. He settled on the passenger side of the front seat. "Command Center. Then on the way home, we'll stop at a pawnshop."

"Pawnshop."

Grover jerked the wheel violently to the left and made the car jump from the curb.

He turned the windshield wipers on. There was a blowing mist.

"How are you the now?" asked Flynn.

The welts on Grover's face appeared purple in the dark car.

"Well," Flynn said to the lack of response. "Perhaps you'd report to me the details of your visit to the home of the widow Geiger in Newton?"

"Nothing there."

"No house? Nothing?"

"No evidence," said Grover.

"Oh, that!"

"Her husband," intoned Grover, "one Raymond Geiger—"

"Juan Raymond Geiger?"

"One Raymond Geiger."

"Oh."

"—was in the shoe business."

"I see," said Flynn.

"He was going to London Monday night, or Tuesday morning, on Zephyr Airways Flight 80."

"Yes."

"To have business meetings in London, and then go on to Frankfurt, Germany. They're a well-to-do family. Big house, Lincoln Continental Mark IV, Mercury station wagon. Lawns. Kids."

"Then why did the boyo insure himself for five thousand dollars before boarding a plane?"

"His wife says he did that all the time. A superstition. For burial expenses."

"More superstition."

"His wife says he made a joke of it—as long as he bought flight insurance and was prepared for the plane to crash, he was sure it wouldn't happen."

Flynn said, "I never thought of flight insurance as an object of comedy. The Flemings had a giggle over it, too. I wonder if the insurance people understand they might as well be in the dial-a-joke business? It would save them from having to pay off on their policies, ever."

"They're not going to, anyway," Grover said.

"Oh?"

"Not right away, anyway. Mrs. Geiger showed me a letter she'd received saying the insurance company was withholding all payments until after the explosion of Flight 80 had been completely investigated."

They were able to move through the tunnel slowly but steadily.

Coming out of the tunnel, Flynn said, quietly, "I wonder if you can tell me what on God's green earth possessed you to go out to Kendall Green and arrest Mrs. Charles Fleming, especially without fair notice to anyone?"

"The same thing that would have possessed you, if you'd had any police training, or experience."

Grover showed his badge to the man in the toll booth, and rolled his window back up.

"And what would that be?" Flynn asked, gently.

"Shit," Grover said. "You and your women."

"Me and my women?"

"A cop is taught, Inspector"—the Sergeant stressed Flynn's rank unkindly—"to keep his emotional cool, his detachment, at all times."

"What a relief," said Flynn.

"The other day at the Fleming broad's house, your eyes were all over her."

"They were."

"You were big-eyed—" Grover expostulated. "Blind!"

" 'Big-eyed blind.' That's as close to poetry as you've ever come, Grover."

"You had the hots for her. Right away. Deny it."

"I don't deny it," said Flynn. "Whatever it is it means."

"Jesus. Pink motorcycle. The wife of a federal judge —herself a college teacher, a consultant for the Boston Police—riding a pink motorcycle. Jesus!"

"Yes," said Flynn. "I was even taken by the pink motorcycle."

"You didn't hear a word she said. She virtually confessed, Frank! You didn't even hear her."

"No. I didn't hear her confess."

"Look, Frank. The Judge was twenty-two years older than his wife. She's thirty-one. He was fifty-three."

"I remember your making some comment on that matter."

"She picks up her husband at his office, drives him to a restaurant on the harbor where they have a late

164

supper and a lot to drink. She drove him to the airport. That's significant. It indicates she'd had less to drink than he had. The old boy had a skinful."

"I see."

Grover placed the car against the curb in front of Zephyr Airways and turned off the ignition.

"Here at the airport she takes out, she thinks she takes out, a half a million dollars' worth of flight insurance on the old boy. Pretending she didn't know there was a one hundred and twenty-five thousand dollar limit on flight insurance may have been part of her blind—so she can have some evidence that she didn't know what she was doing."

"Yes."

A state policeman in a slicker was ambling toward the car.

"She sees his baggage checked through, to be put on the airplane. Even she says that it was she who packed his bag and that he never looked into it."

The trooper banged his fist with extraordinary force against Flynn's window.

Flynn ignored him.

"Then she says she went home and went to bed by herself and the next morning didn't even know the Goddamned plane had exploded all over the Goddamned sky just after takeoff."

Flynn said, "I still don't see any new evidence."

The trooper banged on the car window almost hard enough to break it.

Flynn slowly rolled down the window and looked at the cop.

"What do you want?"

"Get this car out of here! No parking against this curb! Move it!"

Flynn said, "No," and rolled the window back up again, slowly.

He said, "From what you say, Grover, I still don't see what possessed you to arrest the Fleming woman."

Grover said, "Everyone knows the Judge's son is a compulsive gambler."

"Everyone?"

"Everyone."

"I had to find it out, myself."

The trooper was banging his fist, hard, on the top of the car.

"No offense intended, Inspector," Grover said, intending an offense, "but you're not a cop."

"Ach, well. I'll be the first to admit that."

The trooper was banging harder on the car roof.

Flynn rolled down his window halfway.

"Cut that out," he said.

He rolled the window up again.

"Probably the kid, Charles Fleming, Junior, was heavy in debt again."

"I suspect he is," said Flynn.

"Now does it make sense to you?"

"No," Flynn said. "We don't know that Chicky was at the airport. Secondly, Chicky is not the beneficiary of whatever insurance there is. His stepmother is." Flynn began to get out of the car. "I don't think you know anything more than I do, Grover."

"I don't," Grover said. "But you're blind."

"That may be."

The trooper was at the front of the car, copying down the license number.

"Think of a thirty-one-year-old broad with a pink motorcycle and a fifty-three-year-old husband."

"I have been," said Flynn.

He stood on the sidewalk.

Grover shouted at him over the wet roof of the car. "You can't tell me that lady had eyes only for her husband!"

"Maybe not," said Flynn.

The trooper slammed a piece of cardboard against Flynn's chest with incredible force.

"This is the most expensive ticket you've ever gotten, Buddy!"

Flynn let the ticket flutter to the wet sidewalk.

"Now get this car the fuck out of here!"

Flynn said, quietly, "Buzz off."

Over the car roof, Grover said, "Inspector, you still don't get the point."

"Inspector?" said the trooper.

"Mrs. Fleming is thirty-one years old, and her stepson is twenty-six."

"Ah!" said Flynn.

The trooper moved around the front of the car, toward Grover. "Inspector?" he said.

"Ah!" Flynn was looking across the car roof at Grover. "That's what you're thinking?"

"That's it," said Grover.

The trooper said, "Is that Inspector Flynn?"

Grover said, "Aw, fuck off."

Sergeant Richard T. Whelan got into the car, slammed the door, and sat there.

"Humph," Flynn said to the trooper. "That's what he's thinking."

Flynn took a step to the curb and opened the passenger-side car door. He bent over and stuck his head inside the car.

Behind the steering wheel, Grover was staring straight ahead, arms folded across his chest.

"You believe," Flynn said, "that Sassie killed the Judge because she's in love with Chicky?"

167

"I do," said Grover.

"By God. If only the FBI had perceived the full clarity of your thinking, they never would have called me to complain!"

On the sidewalk, Flynn flipped the expensive parking ticket with the edge of his shoe toward the state trooper, and said, "You're littering."

Twenty-four

Flynn found Paul Kirkman in the corridor of the Zephyr Airways Passenger Services offices.

Even at the end of his workday, Kirkman looked freshly pressed and groomed.

"Hello," Flynn said.

"Hello, Inspector."

"I'm not precisely sure what it is I want," Flynn said.

"Who among us mortals does know precisely what it is we want?" Kirkman grinned. "Come into the office."

The fluorescent lights in the little office came on in waves.

On Kirkman's desk was a large cardboard illustration of the interior of a 707.

There were handwritten notes on it, with arrows pointing to some of the seats.

Kirkman stood behind his desk.

Flynn said, "What's this, now?"

"Just something I did." Kirkman flipped the illustration around, so Flynn could read it. "I thought somebody might want it. I noted specifically where some of the passengers were sitting."

"Not all of them?"

"Not all of them had assigned or reserved seats. Just

the first-class passengers did. Unless the coach passengers made a specific request, they were just split into two groups, smoking and nonsmoking."

"I see," said Flynn. "But I see you went to a good school—I can't read your handwriting at all."

Kirkman came around the desk and stood beside Flynn. He ran his index finger down one row of seats. "You see? McCarthy, Hoag, Cairns, I can't read that name myself, Norris, Goldman, Wilcox—"

"I see. And where was Daryl Conover, for instance?"

"Over here. In 15-D."

"How can there be Row 15? There are only twelve rows of seats in first class."

"All the row numbers are double digits on Zephyr aircraft. Per orders of the interior decorator, or the designer, or some other genius. Has something to do with the graphic design of the little number plaques they put on the chair arms, or something. Causes a lot of confusion. People getting on the plane always overshoot their seats and immediately have to start backing up in aisle traffic. The front row of seats on the plane is Row 10."

"So," said Flynn, "the twelve rows in first class are Rows 10 through 21, inclusive?"

"22," said Kirkman. "There is no Row 13."

"Ah!" said Flynn (N. N. 13). "The bad luck number!"

"They were all bad luck numbers, on this flight."

"And where was Leeper sitting?"

"Back here. With his manager. Row 22, Seats C and D. Of course, we don't know which man was in which seat."

"And Judge Fleming?"

"The other side. Up here. Row 14, Seat A."

Flynn said, "Then he was really in Row 13, wasn't he?"

"I guess so. Or Row 4."

"And those three men traveling together?" asked Flynn. "Carson, Bartlett and Abbott?"

"They had these three seats," Kirkman said. "Row 17, Seats A, B, and, across the aisle, C."

"Did they, indeed?"

Kirkman straightened his back. "I don't know why I bothered to do this." Again, he went behind his desk. "Busywork, I guess."

Hat still on, overcoat opened, Flynn was staring into Kirkman's face.

"What's the matter, Inspector? You look like a fly just flew down your throat."

After another moment, still staring at Kirkman, Flynn said, "You're a neat fellow."

"Thank you. Have to be in this job."

"Dealing with passengers all the time," Flynn said. "I think you work hard at keeping up the image of Zephyr Airways."

Kirkman sat down. "I do."

"That's the point," said Flynn. "You were seeing the passengers off on Flight 80 to London at three o'clock in the morning." Flynn put his hands on his hips under his open overcoat. "They had come from four points of the globe, including Boston. At that hour of the morning, your personnel is not at full muster. Right?"

"Right."

"You were standing there, in the departure area, dressed in your Zephyr Airways blazer, and what did you have in your hand?"

"Nothing."

"You had a beer can in your hand."

Kirkman had to think a moment, to remember.

171

"You took a can of beer away from Percy Leeper as he was boarding the plane."

"Yes."

"What did you do with it? You couldn't throw it in a wastebasket because it was open and still had some beer in it."

"Right."

"However, it would be against your instincts, your training—your image, if you will—to stand anywhere in the terminal in your Zephyr Airways blazer with a can of beer in your hand. Right?"

"Of course."

"What did you do with it?"

"I started back to the offices with it. Back here."

"I would say that finding yourself with a can of beer in your hand, you started back to your offices immediately."

"Yes."

"You started back sooner than you normally would have?"

"Yes. I started back immediately."

"Before the door to the airplane was closed?"

"I don't know. I'm not sure."

"Is it possible?"

"Yes."

"All right, Mister Kirkman. You said yesterday that Percy Leeper was the last person to board the airplane."

"I think so. He was about the last to board."

"You also said yesterday it was most likely the stewardesses wouldn't have seen the boarding passes on this flight—that they would have been collected at the entrance to the jetway."

"I think they were."

"So, not having collected the boarding passes, not

being responsible for how many passengers were actually aboard, an empty seat on the plane would not have been particularly noticed by a stewardess?"

"We would have gone looking for a passenger or passengers, Inspector, only if the boarding passes hadn't tallied. And they did." Kirkman glanced at the wall clock. "I don't see what you're driving at, Inspector."

"I'm considering the possibility that someone boarded that plane, and then left it. You wouldn't have seen him. You were already headed back to your office with the can of beer."

"The stewardesses would have seen him."

"I'm not sure of that, either," Flynn said. "You said passengers at that hour of the morning, especially on a transatlantic flight, are apt to be fussy and demanding. There was bound to be some confusion in the aisles. There always is. Secondly, you add the element of Percy Leeper. About the last person to enter the plane, you said. An extremely exuberant, well-built young man, bandages and welts on his face, jumping with joy—in fact, the boyo who had just won the world boxing championship. . . . You can't tell me he didn't turn the head of every stewardess on that plane."

"Inspector, we went over this yesterday. Why would anybody, who was supposed to be aboard that plane and wasn't, not come forward by this time?"

"Precisely."

"Anyway, the CAB and Baumberg say the bomb wasn't planted in the passenger section of the plane. It was planted in a cargo hold."

"I know."

"So why would anybody enter the plane, and then leave it?"

"To give you a boarding pass."

"I don't get it."

173

Flynn straightened the brim of his soft tweed hat.

"It's always dangerous to reduce human beings to pieces of paper," he said. "Some human beings will take advantage of it and present back to you a piece of paper rather than themselves."

"Is that what happened?" Kirkman asked. "Is that what happened here?"

"It may have," answered Flynn. "It may have."

Twenty-five

"There's a pawnshop up here somewhere." Flynn rubbed the condensation off the inside of the windshield with his right fist. In his left hand he held Cocky's map. "There it is. Pull over."

Grover braked hard, nearly in the middle of the street, and turned off the ignition.

"Good," Flynn said. "The devil's own establishment of despair is open for business. I won't be a minute."

On the sidewalk he put his face close to the wet grille over the steamy plate glass of the store front and peered at the collection of cameras, guitars, radios, trumpets, battle ribbons, jewelry, televisions—and violins. He looked especially sharply at a violin at the back of the window display—one without much dust on it.

"I can hear its old sweet song from here," Flynn said to himself.

Just inside the store, he pointed to the violin in the window and said, "I'll see that violin, if you please."

A voice from behind the cage at the back of the shop, an elderly man's voice, said, "Can't you see it from there?"

"I'll have it in my hands."

"That violin's not for sale," the voice creaked.

"You're damned right it's not!"

175

Flynn snatched the violin from the window by its neck and marched with it to the pawnbroker's grille.

"That one," the pawnbroker said, "there's still a ticket out on that one."

"Then what's it doing in the window?"

Through the grille Flynn could see a white-haired little man in a white shirt too big for him, stacking coins on the counter. The little man shrugged.

"This is my son's violin," said Flynn.

The little man shrugged again. "It is if he brings the pawn ticket back. With money."

"And how much money do you expect?"

The man studied the coded ticket dangling from the neck of the violin through the grille. "A hundred dollars for that one."

"Are you telling me you lent out a hundred dollars on this violin?"

"Sure. It's a good violin. Play it a little."

"Where's the bow?"

"Pick it a little."

Flynn sounded the A-string with his thumbnail.

"You don't know how to play the violin," the pawnbroker said, "so you pick it a little. You don't know how to pick, either."

"By God, he's not only a pawnbroker, but a music critic to boot!"

"Put the violin back in the window, will you, Mister? It's not for sale yet."

"Actually," said Flynn. "I'm taking it home with me."

The little man looked at him owlishly through the grille.

"Without," Flynn added, "paying you a dime."

"Look, Mister. Whose fault is it your son pawned his violin to me?"

176

"My son!" Flynn pretended astonishment. "You mean the kid who pawned this violin was redheaded?"

The pawnbroker studied Flynn's own thick brown hair.

"Yes," he said. "He was."

"Good!" Flynn pretended relief. "My son is blond."

The old man's gaze went into Flynn's eyes.

"You bought stolen property," said Flynn.

"Mister, there happens to be a law in this state protecting pawnbrokers from charges of buying stolen property."

"There is?"

"Everything we buy, everything we lend money out on—we can't be sure the person selling the goods to us actually owns it."

"There's entirely too much law," said Flynn.

At the side of the shop were a half-dozen violin cases on the floor.

Flynn had to study them only a moment before picking out Randy's and bringing it to the cage.

"Now," said Flynn, "have I ever been in this pawnshop before?"

"Maybe," the old man said.

"Have I been in this pawnshop at any time since this violin case has been here?"

"Maybe."

"Did the violin in my right hand enter this pawnshop in the violin case in my left hand?"

"Maybe."

"What was the name of the person who pawned this violin?"

"I don't know."

"You're not required to ask?"

"No."

"The marvelous protection of the law!" scoffed

Flynn. "Obviously you opened the violin case to take the violin out."

"Maybe," answered the little old man.

"And you saw that on the inside lid of this violin case, printed in big block letters, are the initials 'R.F.'?"

The pawnbroker said nothing.

Putting the violin on the shelf, Flynn opened the violin case.

On the inside lid, printed in blue block letters between the bows, were the initials 'R.F.'

"Did you inquire of the person who pawned this violin if his initials were 'R.F.'?"

He turned the violin case so the man could see the initials clearly.

"They might have been the initials of a previous owner," said the pawnbroker.

"Indeed they are," said Flynn, putting the violin into the case. "The previous and present owner. You did not take ordinary precautions to guarantee that you were not buying stolen property."

"I don't have to," the pawnbroker said. "The law—"

"The hell with the law!" said Boston Police Inspector Francis Xavier Flynn. "There's entirely too much of it!"

"Mister," the little old pawnbroker said, "if you try to walk out of here with that violin, I'll call the police on you."

"I am the police!" said Boston Police Inspector Francis Xavier Flynn.

The pawnbroker blinked at him.

"I have identification here somewhere."

Flynn rummaged through his pockets.

He showed the pawnbroker his badge through the grille.

"You're Inspector Flynn? I've read about you in the newspapers."

"You're about to read about yourself in the newspapers! You not only knowingly bought stolen property, you bought it from a minor!"

Again the man blinked at him.

"You said it was a boy who sold you this violin."

"Maybe."

"You will please describe the boy to me. Was he redheaded?"

The pawnbroker blinked.

"Of course he wasn't redheaded," said Flynn. "That would make it much too easy for me. Redheads learn early enough in life never to commit crimes in front of witnesses. What did the boy look like?"

"Just a boy."

"Was he dark or light?"

"White boy. Dark hair."

"How old was he?"

"Eighteen."

"Was he fifteen?"

"Maybe."

"Was he a big kid or a little kid?"

"Big kid. Not tall. Heavyset."

"Any distinguishing features?" rolled Flynn.

"He was just a kid, Inspector. A clean-looking kid. His hair was brushed."

"Wonder of wonders," said Flynn. "Color of eyes?"

"I don't know."

"Scars or marks on his face?"

"No. Chipped tooth. Here in front." The pawnbroker pointed to the front of his own dentures.

"Right in front there, eh?" Flynn studied the pawnbroker's dentures. "One tooth or two teeth?"

"Two. I think."

"Now, that's curious," said Flynn. "Would you tell me how you happen to remember such a thing as that?"

"He was a clean-looking kid, Inspector. He looked like he had been well taken care of. But he had these chipped teeth, right in front."

"I see," said Flynn. "Now surely that's a thought process you'd more likely have toward a boy of fifteen than a boy of eighteen?"

The pawnbroker looked at the coins on his counter. "Maybe."

Flynn lifted the violin case off the counter.

He said, "Thank you for your cooperation."

The pawnbroker shrugged.

Grover had not moved the car from the near center of the street.

Flynn put the violin on the back seat.

Getting into the front seat, Flynn said, "Now, if you'd drop me home?"

Grover stamped so heavily on the accelerator the car slipped on the wet pavement.

"Shit!" he said. "Another violin!"

Twenty-six

After washing, Flynn settled himself at the head of the dining table.

"Did the boys call in?"

Elsbeth was ladling out the soup.

"Todd at five minutes to four. Randy at quarter past."

Flynn put his napkin in his lap.

"Anything to report?"

"Just that they're all right."

"Good."

Flynn tasted Elsbeth's good back-of-the-stove soup. Different every night.

"I found Randy's violin," Flynn said. "In a pawnshop. But I forgot and left it in the car."

He spread cream cheese on a cracker.

"Would you believe," Flynn said, "that Ifadi Minister of the Exchequer, Rashin al Khatid, described as an unsophisticated man, flew to London on Zephyr Airways Flight 80, in the first-class compartment, Row 17, Seat A, B, or C?"

Elsbeth said, "That's ridiculous."

At the other end of the table, Elsbeth tasted the soup herself.

"Isn't it just?" said Flynn.

"Needs salt," Elsbeth said. "Jenny, pass the salt to your father."

Twenty-seven

Flynn said, slowly, very distinctly, "Mihson Taha?"

The man who had opened the door to the hotel suite stared at Flynn.

His white shirt was buttoned at the throat, but he was without a necktie.

He was a strong-looking, heavy-shouldered man with a thickly muscled neck.

He would not be the secretary.

"No," said Flynn. "You're Nazim Salem Zoyad."

The man began to swing the door to slam it in Flynn's face.

Flynn kicked the middle of the door with the flat of his foot, hard.

The door jerked out of Nazim Salem Zoyad's hand and hit him in the face, sending him staggering back into the living room.

Flynn stepped into the living room of the suite.

"Excuse me," he said. "I need to see the Minister. The name's Flynn."

He had spent the entire morning visiting the security offices of various upper-class Boston hotels, showing his passport photos of Mihson Taha, Nazim Salem Zoyad and Rashin al Khatid, asking the simple question, "Did three men, traveling together, check into your

182

hotel, under any names whatsoever, anytime Tuesday, including before dawn?"

Registries had to be checked, desk clerks and bell-hops interviewed.

At one hotel, Flynn found himself confronting the president of a Canadian bank chain, his secretary and chauffeur.

Finally, at Boston's newest expensive hotel, the Royale, the deskman had been able to confirm that three men, traveling together, had checked into a suite between three-thirty and four Tuesday morning. No one there could identify them from Flynn's photos. The men had taken all their meals in the suite.

Their names, according to the registry card, were Desmond, Edwards, and Francini.

"Ah, la," said Flynn. "We have them."

It then took Flynn a few moments to dissuade the Hotel Royale security officer from accompanying him to the suite.

Flynn did not state the reason for his interest in the men.

It appeared to be a suite with a living room, two bedrooms, and a bath. The door to one of the bedrooms was open, showing twin, unmade beds.

The door to the other bedroom was closed.

A man slighter than Nazim Salem Zoyad, dressed in jacket and tie, stood up from the divan. He had been looking at a copy of *Playboy* magazine.

"You're Mihson Taha," Flynn said.

"And who might you be, sir?"

"I might be anybody," said Flynn. "But I ain't."

As Flynn was opening the bedroom door, Mihson Taha grabbed him by the shoulders.

Flynn sent the heel of his right shoe smartly against the man's shin.

183

The man removed his hands from Flynn's shoulders instantly.

Rashin al Khatid, Minister of the Exchequer of the Republic of Ifad, was sitting up on a double bed, well-bolstered by pillows, reading an old, leather-bound book.

"Good day, Your Excellency." Flynn closed the door firmly behind him. "Delighted I am to find you in the pink."

His Excellency looked at Flynn over the top of the book, but said nothing.

He, too, was dressed in a white business shirt, buttoned at the throat.

Flynn had seen no luggage in the suite.

The luggage had gone on the airplane.

As Flynn moved to the foot of the bed, the door opened.

Quietly, Nazim Salem Zoyad and Mihson Taha entered.

Mihson Taha stood to one side, rubbing his shin.

Flynn said, "It's my sad duty to investigate the explosion of Zephyr Airways Flight 80 to London, this last Tuesday."

"A regrettable incident," said the Minister, "in the long and otherwise superior history of commercial aviation."

"A blotch," agreed Flynn. "A veritable blotch."

The Minister put his book down on his stomach.

"I had the wisdom," he said, "to not partake in the flight myself."

"I know," said Flynn.

"We boarded the airplane in good faith," continued the Minister wearily, "secure in our belief proper and satisfactory arrangements had been made for us, but almost immediately discovered such was not the case."

184

"Your seats were in Row 17," said Flynn.

"Yes. The young ladies who were in charge of amenities said they could do nothing to help us change our seats, as we were three people, traveling together. One young lady, stewardess, said she might be able to help us change our seats after the plane had taken off, but by then I knew, of course, it would be too late. We had difficulty engaging the attention of any of the young ladies as a wild young man entered the plane just after us, with bandages on his face, striking the air with his fists, saying with boring repetition but undeniable exuberance the word 'peppermint.' "

"So you left the plane," said Flynn.

"I had no choice," said the Minister, "but to make such a decision. Seventeen is recognized as the most unlucky number, in my part of the world."

"Like our number thirteen," said Flynn.

"Your regard for the number thirteen," sighed the Minister, "is based on a complete misperception."

"I've always thought so," Flynn said.

"I would be unwilling to fly on an airplane which even had a Row 17, if I knew it. For Zephyr Airways to present to me an airplane containing a Row 17 indicates not only foolhardiness on their part but a most undiplomatic insensitivity to the wisdom of my people. A complete insult to us." His Excellency smiled at his aide. "I am most grateful to my secretary for pointing out to me the number given our row. Otherwise I might not have noticed. I would not expect such an affront."

"Well," Flynn said to the Minister, "you're every bit the boyo I expected you to be."

"Can you call me wrong?" asked the Minister. "If I had sat in that seat I would be dead now."

"Bless my nose, the plane crashed anyway," said Flynn.

"But I was not on it."

"And Row 17 was actually Row 7, if you take your count from number one, or Row 16, if you begin with ten and leave out thirteen, as they did; a hundred and fifteen people were blown to death in midair, it now appears, but never-the-mind, never-the-mind, Your Excellency's life has been spared by wisdom, sharp observation, and the powers-that-be."

The Minister of the Exchequer dipped his head in solemn acknowledgment of Flynn's conclusion.

"My curiosity is," said Flynn, "why you're keeping your being alive a secret all this while? Or am I about to be told it was curiosity that extinguished the tom-cat?"

"Are we keeping it a secret?"

"I've seen few of your vital signs displayed on the television screen."

"We're on a highly secret diplomatic mission, Mister um-ah—"

"Francis Xavier Flynn."

"Mister Francis Xavier Flynn. Your Department of State has extended to us, what shall we say, special passports, so that our visit here, to accomplish our most delicate and complex mission while enjoying the benefit of anonymity—"

"I know about the phony passports," said Flynn. "I've even heard a word or two about your delicate mission."

"Then you understand our inability to make joyous announcements concerning our miraculous—as you might say—preservation from disaster."

"Oof," said Flynn. "The man does go on. Tell me, you blithering, blathering fig sprig, have you let anyone at all in on the secret that you're still drawing breath?"

The Minister's eyes narrowed.

"We have made the proper notification to our capital."

"And what did they say?" asked Flynn. "Did a cheer go up from the streets?"

"We are awaiting instructions."

" 'Awaiting instructions,' is it? And has anyone thought to notify the most generous and considerate United States Department of State that holders of phony passports in the names of Abbott, Barlett, and Carson are now taking in breath under the names of Desmond, Edwards, and Francini?"

"Such a step, when and if taken, will be taken by our capital," said Rashin al Khatid.

"So far, you know," Flynn winked at the Minister of the Exchequer, "your capital has said nothing."

A crease appeared momentarily in the Minister's forehead.

"The right decision will be attained by my government, at the right time, Mister Xavier Flynn."

"Sure, sure," said Flynn. "In the meantime, we've got the Minister of the Exchequer of the Republic of Ifad miraculously risen from the dead living on the fourteenth floor of a Boston hotel—actually, the thirteenth floor, I'll have you know—under three phony passports and six phony names. By the way, where did you get that book you're reading, in Arabic?"

The Minister glanced at his bodyguard before answering.

"It was in my attaché case."

"Your attaché case did not go down with the plane?"

"No. I had it with me."

"Your papers were saved?"

187

Again the Minister hesitated. "Yes."

"Miracles bloom in the spring."

At the bedroom door, Flynn said, "I'll use your phone, if you don't mind. I'm having a police guard put on the door of your suite twenty-four hours a day. No one, including yourselves, is going to enter or leave this suite without my knowledge and permission."

From his bed, the Minister of the Exchequer said, "Are we being placed under guard, Mister Xavier Flynn?"

"Protected," said Flynn. "You're being heavily protected."

Twenty-eight

"What's that, now?"

Flynn leaned forward, putting his eyes close to the steamy, rain-specked car windshield.

A crowd was collected on the steps of the Old Records Building on Craigie Lane. Television trucks from three networks, cars emblazoned with the names of various newspapers clogged the streets. Some of the people held television cameras; others held still cameras; still others, microphones.

On the steps of the Old Records Building stood Baird (Robert Cullen) Hastings, facing the crowd, looking lean and somber, hands in the pockets of a dark overcoat, collar turned up.

"Here," Flynn said to Grover. "Let me out. I've got to see this."

Flynn turned up his own coat collar and stood in the crowd.

Hastings was answering a question.

"I've not been charged with murder," Hastings said. "Mass murder. As far as I know, I'm not being charged with this most heinous deed. I have been questioned. Extensively. By the police."

Flynn couldn't hear the next question.

"Yes," said Baird Hastings. "I have been told that I am a prime suspect in this case."

Nor could Flynn hear the next question.

"Of course. I admit it," was the answer. "When I was a kid in the Army I was trained to deal with explosive materials. I was trained in demolition."

"Who told you you're a prime suspect?"

"Inspector Flynn."

As he was standing behind the reporters, most of their questions were blown out of Flynn's hearing.

"No, I do not now have access to dynamite or any other explosive materials," Hastings said.

In answer to the next question, he said, "Yes, it is true. Within this period of time, recently, I bought some dynamite. I had a license to use it. I mean, to buy it and use it. I used it to get rid of some rocks in my backyard."

"Who says you didn't have some left?"

"Absolutely not. I used all the dynamite to blow up the rocks. You're invited to my place anytime. You can take pictures of the evidence. You can see what I've done."

"How can we see rocks that aren't there anymore?"

"Mister Hastings, if you used all the dynamite to blow up the rocks, you must have known enough to buy exactly what you needed. I mean, known enough about dynamite."

"Of course. Anyhow, dynamite isn't the sort of thing you leave lying around."

"Therefore, you must have a pretty good idea of how much dynamite you'd need to blow up a 707."

Hastings shrugged. "Not much."

"Not much of an idea, or not much dynamite?"

"Not much dynamite. It wouldn't take much dynamite to blow up an airplane."

Another question was blown away on the wind.

Hastings pinched the top of his nose.

"I loved that man. Daryl Conover was one of the all-time great actors—and not just in the Shakespearean field. Maybe the greatest." Hastings' hand brushed his right eyelid. His voice dropped. "He was also a very dear friend."

"Is it true you and he had a big fight on opening night?"

"Of course not."

"Then why did he leave the show?"

"He was upset," Hastings said. "Very upset that night. Something about taxes. English taxes."

"Is that why he went home? Back to England? To pay his taxes?"

Hastings' eyes fell on Flynn in the crowd.

Quickly, Hastings looked away.

He faltered before answering the question.

"Conover was not leaving my production of *Hamlet* for good. He just had some personal problems. Something about English taxes. We were going to work something out."

Flynn began moving around the crowd, to enter the building.

As he was climbing the steps, collar up, hat brim down, very much in the background, he heard Hastings saying, "Yes. I am here to be further questioned. I mean, questioned further. By the police. By . . . Inspector Flynn."

Alone in his office, wishing he had taken time to have lunch at the hotel, Flynn listened on the telephone to the voice of John Roy Priddy—N. N. Zero.

"I have terrible news for you, Frank."

"Oh?"

"Yes. Always hate to be the bearer of sad tidings."

191

"And you don't enjoy the dragging out of your giving of the bad news, either, do you?"

"A friend of yours is dead, Frank."

"And who might that be?"

"Are you sure you can take bad news?"

"I'll try to be brave."

"Are you sitting down, Frank?"

"I'm jumping with anticipation. There might have been a will."

"I have two dispatches from Ainslee, capital of the Republic of Ifad."

"No! You don't say."

"I do."

"You can't!"

"The first one reads, and I'm reading it to you: 'The Government of the Republic of Ifad—' "

"It can't be."

" '—reports, with sorrow, the death of the Minister of the Exchequer, Rashin al Khatid, at the age of forty-six.' "

"Poor man. Did he suffer long?"

" 'The Minister's death was sudden, of an apparent heart attack, as he worked at his desk late last night.' "

"He died serving his country," said Flynn.

"Do you need more? The report goes on to say the Minister had been in office only six weeks—"

"Six weeks?"

"Yes."

Flynn said, "He is risen."

"What?"

"At the moment he's on the fourteenth floor of a Boston hotel."

"Who is?"

"Rashin al Khatid. Also Nazim Salem Zoyad. Also Mihson Taha."

"Are you serious?"

"Yes. I just left them."

"What are they doing there?"

"I doubt they're waiting for a fourth for bridge."

"They never got on the airplane?"

"They got on it, but they got off again. Which is why we all thought they were on it. They had handed in their boarding passes. The airlines had the insensitivity to try to seat His Excellency and aides in Row 17."

"Oh."

"We all make our social gaffes, on occasion. Even airlines."

"So the buggers just got off the plane? Didn't anybody see them?"

"Apparently not."

"Why haven't they said anything?"

"They are awaiting instructions from their capital."

"Uh! Sounds like they've had 'em! It's called abandonment of personnel, Frank."

"I seem to remember it happening to me once. But I wouldn't think of reminding you of it, sir."

"What are we going to do with them?"

"At the moment they are being protected by Boston's finest. I have a cop at their door."

"Does anybody else know about this?"

"No."

"Good. Keep it that way. Do you want to hear the second dispatch?"

"Especially if it is as funny as the first."

"This isn't an official dispatch. It's from our own people in Ifad."

"Sir, there's only so much anticipation I can take in a day."

"It reports that China is selling Ifad half a billion dollars in arms."

Flynn's eyes moved along all four sides of his desk blotter. They then reversed direction and squared his blotter again.

"Frank? Are you there?"

"I think so," said Flynn. "But I'm not entirely sure. Can the report be correct?"

"It can be correct," said N. N. Zero. "It can also be incorrect."

"Tell me, sir. Do we still have a Chinese translator in Montreal, Canada?"

"Yes."

"At home at the same address?"

"Yes. Do you want to see him?"

"I'm not sure," said Flynn. "At the moment, I'm not sure of anything."

"I'm glad you're involved in this case, Frank."

"It was a Russian submarine that was pursued out of Massachusetts Bay, was it not? Russian, that is, not Chinese?"

"Right. Russian."

"This case," said Flynn, "has as many dangling loose ends as your average English sheep dog."

"That's what makes it interesting. Right, Frank?"

". . . Right."

"I don't know my next move."

Flynn was standing over the chessboard, staring at it.

He had heard Cocky enter the office, dragging one foot behind him.

Cocky looked from the chessboard to Flynn. "You don't?"

"I do not," said Flynn. "I do not know what my next move is. Methinks it will take some thinking."

Cocky said, "Mister Baird Hastings is here to see you."

"I know. I read about it in the newspapers. Or, I'm about to."

"Shall I let him in?"

"Go ahead, Cocky. We all work our way toward salvation with fear and trembling. After he goes, I'm leaving the office myself. I intend to visit Cartwright School this afternoon. A little rest and relaxation, if you take my meaning."

Cocky chuckled. "Your next move is obvious, Inspector."

"Is it? Is it though?"

When Baird Hastings entered Flynn's office his overcoat was open, but his hands were still in his pockets.

He stood in the middle of the room, and said nothing.

Flynn said, "You make a pretty good case against yourself. I couldn't have done better myself. If I were given to holding press conferences, that is."

Hastings' lips turned into a slight smile.

Flynn said, "Would you believe I don't have any more 'extensive questioning' for you at the moment? I hate to disappoint your audience and all that—"

"I told you, Inspector, I will stop at nothing to keep my production of *Hamlet* from closing, even without Daryl Conover."

"At nothing?"

"At nothing—even including implicating myself in one of history's worst crimes."

" 'At nothing,' Mister Hastings, means you might even have committed the crime."

"There are too many people whose livings and careers depend on the show's staying open—even if that shithead, Conover, did walk off."

" 'Shithead,' is it now? 'I loved that man,' " Flynn quoted. " 'Daryl Conover was one of the all-time great actors—and not just in the Shakespearean field. Maybe the greatest.' " Flynn dropped his voice dramatically. " 'He was also my very dear friend.' Did you write all that yourself?"

"You're a quick study, Inspector."

"Bless my Irish ears. They never miss an intonation. Of course, you forgot to mention that your own living and career depend on that show's staying open. With Daryl Conover. Or without him."

"I've been honest about that."

"To me, you have."

"The press conference I just gave will fill the house and maybe even get us into New York."

"I figured that's what you were doing. Pardon me if I'm wrong, but I think in your business it's called a cheap publicity stunt. Have I got it right?"

"Look. People will come to the theater now hoping to get a glimpse of me. Me: prime suspect. They'll sit there watching Rod fucking up *Hamlet* but they'll actually be seeing Daryl Conover, mourning him, consoling themselves with the idea that no one could compare with him anyway."

"And all this time," said Flynn, "you'll be sulking around the theater competing with Hamlet's father, a veritable wraith yourself, sad and nervous, allowing people to perturb themselves with the thought that you actually might have killed Daryl Conover and a hundred and seventeen other people. You have your talents, Mister Hastings."

Baird Hastings looked at the floor.

And then looked up at Flynn.

"Do you blame me?"

Flynn said, "I think it may be one of the cleverest efforts to remove suspicion from a prime suspect I've ever had the pleasure of witnessing."

196

Twenty-nine

"Now look at this incredible thing, will you?"

Flynn pretended to be surprised at finding the pin Irwin Maurice Fletcher had sent Jenny in his vest pocket.

Indifferently he held it out to the boy nearest him, who took it gingerly.

"Is it real?"

"It is."

The hockey team of Cartwright School had come off the ice ten or fifteen minutes before (Flynn had watched their practice for a half-hour and then had spent a few moments saying what he hoped were the right enthusiastic things to the coach concerning the team's chances for the rest of the season) and stripped their smelly uniforms off their sweaty bodies, jammed them into smelly lockers, slamming the light steel, air-vented doors, shouting back and forth to each other, as if decibels could overcome wretched smells.

Their winter-white skin at first was flushed from their exercise; as they ambled back from their showers, their skin was a different kind of red, from soap and hot water.

Almost to a man they pulled their clothes on over wet skin. Their major efforts went to drying and arranging their hair.

Three of the hockey players had visible dental problems. One had an upper tooth missing. (He returned from the shower room wearing a false tooth.) A second had a lower front tooth chipped. A third had two upper teeth chipped.

Jenny's pin was being handed from boy to boy.

"Think of anybody giving such a thing to a twelve-year-old girl," Flynn said.

"Who? Someone gave it to Jenny?"

"Yes."

"What's the red stuff?" asked one.

"Ruby," said Flynn. "Rubies."

"My sister has a pin like that," said a boy.

"She has not," said another.

Flynn said, "She has not."

He turned his back on the boys and went to the water bubbler and had a long drink.

When he turned around, the pin was nowhere in sight.

The boy to whom he had handed it was pulling on his sweater. He was saying, "You rest on your skates like Bobby Orr, Tony. Too bad you can't do anything else like he did."

By the door, a boy was zipping up his ski parka.

It was the boy with the chipped upper teeth.

He took his schoolbooks from a bench, opened the door with his free hand, and, without saying anything to anybody, went through the door, alone.

Moving very slowly through the confusion of chunky boys pulling on winter clothing, Flynn followed.

Thirty

He waited until the boy looked over his shoulder and saw Flynn following him before he said anything.

In the dark, the whites of the boy's eyes seemed too large.

Flynn said, quietly, "Wait up, lad. I'll walk along home with you."

The boy stopped. He turned halfway.

They were under a street light.

"How do you know which direction I'm going?"

The boy's voice was huskier than Flynn expected.

"Whichever way you go, lad, I can tell you you're going in the wrong direction."

The boy was taking rapid, short breaths.

Facing the boy under the street light, Flynn said, "You're a thief."

The boy's body braced to run.

Flynn put his hand on the boy's shoulder and squeezed it, just once, to show the boy Flynn could restrain him.

The boy turned his face up to Flynn.

"You've no right—"

Flynn unzipped the lower right pocket of the boy's ski parka and inserted his left hand.

He withdrew Jenny's pin from the pocket.

He held it up in front of the boy's face, letting it reflect the street light.

The boy wouldn't look at it.

"Maybe you're not a thief," said Flynn, gently. "But lately you've been doing a whale of a lot of stealing."

Flynn dropped the pin into a pocket of his own overcoat.

He let go of the boy.

"What's your name, lad?"

"Are you Todd Flynn's father?"

"I am."

"Shit."

"So you might as well tell me your name."

"What are you going to do about it? I mean, about my taking the pin?"

Flynn said, "I'm going to try to puzzle out with you why it's happening. Why you're stealing."

"Are you going to turn me in? I mean, to the cops?"

Flynn smiled.

"Jesus." The boy looked sickly at the sidewalk. "You are a cop. Inspector Flynn. Shit!"

"Enough of all that now. Are you going to tell me your name?"

The boy looked back at the school gates. "Cary," he said. He blinked. "Cary Dickerman. What are you going to do?"

Flynn said, "I thought we'd have a walk-and-talk. How far from here do you live?"

"Two blocks."

"Come on, lad. We'll walk and you talk."

The man and the boy walked down the dark winter sidewalk together.

After a few paces, Flynn asked, "Can you tell me why you're stealing everything that isn't screwed to the floor?"

"What else am I supposed to do?"

"I never heard anybody say you're 'supposed to' steal."

"Money." Cary shrugged.

Flynn said nothing.

Cary changed his schoolbooks from one hip to the other.

Then he changed them back again.

"Dad's gone," he said.

Flynn said, "I'm sorry to hear that."

Breathing badly, speaking quickly, in a voice higher than the voice he had been using, Cary said, "After Christmas. He couldn't take it anymore. He didn't know what to do. I don't know where he is. He tried. He really tried. He blamed himself. He said it was all his fault. He just didn't know what to do. He didn't trust himself anymore. He—he didn't even trust himself with me. He left me. The poor guy. He was reeling."

They were walking slowly.

"The house," Cary said. "I don't even know about things like mortgages, and—and banks. There has to be food. I paid the oil bill."

Flynn put his hand on the boy's shoulder.

"I keep expecting him back."

The boy dodged out from under Flynn's hand.

"I went to the electric company and the telephone company. I gave them cash. I haven't done anything about tuition. I don't even know how much it is."

Walking the next block, the boy's breathing became more even.

"Dad just didn't know what to do. He was hurt. Disappointed. He couldn't handle it."

Cary Dickerman stopped outside a modest brick house.

"Is this where you live?"

"Yes."

There was a faint light in one room.

"May I come in?"

The boy studied Flynn's face.

"Do you want to?"

"Yes."

Cary shrugged and went up the steps.

He took a house key from his back pocket and opened the front door.

Flynn followed him inside.

The boy was struggling to get the key out of the lock.

A woman sat in a straight kitchen chair in the living room, ankles crossed, hands folded in her lap.

Beside her, on an overturned wooden grapefruit crate, were a full ashtray and a few glasses.

The only light in the room came from a table lamp, which was on the floor, at some distance from her.

The room had no other furniture.

The woman's hair was neatly combed.

Her eyes in that light seemed to be without pupils —they were entirely gray.

Flynn remained in the living room doorway.

Looking at him, the woman said, "Is . . . that . . . Cary . . . you . . . Cary . . . ?"

Cary had closed the front door.

He stood in the front hall, looking at his mother in the living room.

"There used to be a piano," he said.

"Do you have any idea what it is she takes?" Flynn asked.

"No." Cary leaned against the newel post. "And I don't know where she gets it. And I don't know where she keeps it. And I don't know how she takes it, or when she takes it."

"I see," Flynn said. "I should know more about this, but I don't. Tell me, lad, can you get your own supper?"

"Sure." Cary nodded at his mother. "She also drinks. She used to be a nice mother."

"What will you do with her? Can you put her to bed?"

"No. I'll have to leave her there. I'll just take away her cigarettes. And matches. So she won't burn down what's left of the house. She does everything," Cary said. "She drinks and smokes and shoots up and pops pills and whatever else. She's a beaut."

The boy sighed and sat on the second stair.

"Tell me, son," Flynn said. "Why haven't you told anyone about this?"

"It's not exactly something you brag about."

"I know, but—your mother's sick, Cary. Do you understand that much?"

Cary shook his head.

"Does the Dickerman family belong to a church?"

"Methodist. Wentworth-Methodist Church. Haven't gone for a long time, of course."

Flynn said, "You know, lad, I suspect you wish you had been caught stealing long before now. Is that true?"

Cary stood up.

He said, "I've got homework to do."

He picked his books up off the stairs.

"By the way," Flynn said, "How much did the pawnbroker give you for Randy's violin?"

"Twenty dollars," Cary said. He shrugged. "He knew I stole it."

Flynn watched the boy climb the stairs, carrying both his schoolbooks and his pride, neatly.

Then Flynn let himself out.

Thirty-one

"Da?"

"Good evening, Randy." Flynn looked at his watch. It was quarter-past-two. "Good morning."

Flynn had staggered out to the telephone in the hall on bare feet. He took a step sideways, to stand on the hall rug.

"I've found the HSL."

"Really? Good lad! Where are they?"

"1319 Fosburg Street."

"Are you there now?"

"I'm in a phone booth on the street. Outside Hippo's liquor store."

"I've got it. Can you fill me in? How many are they, who are they—"

"You'll be surprised."

"Try me."

"Would you believe the Human Surplus League is one nutty guy with a typewriter and a can of spray paint?"

"I'd believe anything."

"He's starkers, Da. He didn't blow up any airplane."

"Why do you say that?"

"He couldn't organize it. He couldn't organize himself. I tell you, Da, he's a basket case. A raving lunatic."

"Are you sure he's not one of a group?"

"He's the group, the whole group. This kid—one of the runaways I've been crashing with—he brought me over."

"How did he know about the HSL?"

"Everybody in Cambridge knows about Jade. He's a local character."

"Everybody but the police."

"Oh, the police must know about him. They just wouldn't think of turning him in. He's harmless."

"He calls himself 'Jade'?"

"Yeah. I've been talking to him since about eleven o'clock. Listening to his raving."

"Did he say anything about the airplane?"

"He's been lecturing us about minks."

"Minks?"

"Yeah, you know those little animals you make coats out of."

"I never have."

"Jade says they swallow their young, at the slightest frightening noise."

"And is that what everybody in Boston was supposed to do when the airplane exploded?"

"He didn't blow up the airplane, Da."

"Is the other kid still with you?"

"No. I was waiting for him to leave before calling you."

"Okay, Randy. You stay there. Outside the liquor store. Hippo's, is it called? I'll get cooperation from the Cambridge police and get there as soon as I can."

"Take your time, Da. Have a cup of Eyebright before you come, if you want."

"That's kind of you, lad. See you soon."

"Are you bringing Grover?"

"Under the circumstances I think I'll leave Grover

in his kennel—where I hope he is. His voice still rises when he mentions your name. Although, for the life of me, I can't think why."

Randy guffawed into the phone.

"Are you all right yourself?"

"Sure."

"All right, Randy. I'll be there in a few minutes."

"I'm hungry," Randy said.

"What?"

"I'm hungry!"

Flynn said, "I've never known you when you weren't."

Flynn let the phone ring a dozen times.

"Hello?"

"Sassie?"

"Who is it?"

"Frank Flynn, Sassie. Can you wake up?"

"I don't think so. I took one of those pills. A Sessonal. I mean, a Seconal. What time is it?"

"Twenty-five minutes to three in the morning. Shall I sing you a few bars of 'Frère Jacques'?"

"Is Chicky all right?"

"Why do you ask?"

"Why are you calling me at two-thirty in the morning?"

"I want you to meet me at 1319 Fosburg Street in Cambridge as soon as you can."

"What?"

"Look for Hippo's liquor store. It's near that."

"Frank, really! If this is your idea of impetuously arranging an assignation—"

"Ach, quit! It's a police matter."

"I'll say it is—calling me at two-thirty in the morning."

"We've found the HSL."

"The Human Surplus League?"

"You've got it."

"Listen, Frank, I also don't want to have anything to do with storming a place with tear gas and machine guns and bazookas! Not my line of work at all."

"I find you talk a lot in your sleep."

"You heard me."

"I did. Now, would you pull on your bloomers and get yourself into Cambridge as fast as you can, please? Use your pink motorcycle, why don't you?"

"Frank—"

"I promise you, there won't be a bazooka in sight; not even a machine gun."

"No tear gas?"

"We'll leave Cambridge as dry-eyed as we found it."

"All right. It's a good thing I know you don't drink. What's the number on Fosburg Street?"

"1319. Near Hippo's liquor store. Got it?"

"Yes."

"Good," Flynn said. "Nice doing business with you."

Thirty-two

"SQUONK!" yelled the man, threateningly.

He held them all at bay in the doorway of his filthy, near-empty loft on the second floor of 1319 Fosburg Street, with a can of spray paint.

As soon as any of them—either of the two Cambridge detectives, Flynn or Sassie Fleming, Randy, all huddled in the door—began to say anything or move forward, the man calling himself Jade, doing business as the Human Surplus League, would strike a dueling pose and press his button. Black paint would spray from the nozzle, fragment in the air, and drift to the floor. They were well out of range.

Jade had been lecturing them for some time.

"Kill lovingly! I say. Kill lovingly! Before it is too late to kill lovingly! Soon you will be out of space. Soon you will be out of food. Soon you will be out of water. Soon you will be out of air. Then will come Armageddon! Brother will kill brother, and father child, not in love, but in hatred, not in kindness, but in greed! In greed for space, for food, for water, for air!"

Flynn kept stepping forward and back, each time triggering another squirt of black paint.

Soon, he knew, the can would be empty.

"Slaughter the innocents, now! Slaughter them innocently! Let nothing stop you from loving murder!"

Skinny Jade, barefooted in the freezing loft, wore narrow black trousers and a paint-smeared once-white T-shirt. His head was almost completely enveloped in long, curly, greasy black hair. The lenses of his glasses were almost as thick as ice cubes; behind them, his eyes were frantic, intense.

"As, at one time in ancient history, when there was work to be done—work that could be done—animals bred, fields sown, and forests felled, there was a need for people to populate the earth, it was right, it was moral to bring people into the world. But now, now! Oh, God, now! It is right, it is moral to take as many people off the world with you as you can." (Squirt.) "Don't approach me! I am your prophet!"

On a card table in the loft was an International Business Machines office-size typewriter. There was no accompanying chair.

Flat on the floor and leaning against the walls were spray-painted posters, mostly made from the sides of cardboard boxes. "KILL THY NEIGHBOR!" "MASS PRODUCTION / MASS MURDER!" "MURDER WITHOUT PREJUDICE!" "DO YOUR BIT—KILL SOMEONE TODAY!" Some of the posters were nicely decorated, in reds and greens.

In one corner of the loft, thick newspaper sections had been laid down. They were urine-soaked. Excrement rested on top of the pile.

The smell of the paint shot at them relieved the noses of everyone in the doorway.

"Listen to the words of Heraclitus, and practice the noble arts of war!" (Squirt.) "Take your young, your healthy, your strong—your best—and run them against each other's swords!" (Squirt.) "Especially the young, the unformed and unfucked! Use them as cannon fodder! Destroy them before they destroy you, before they destroy life—before they procreate!"

When Flynn had arrived on Fosburg Street, Randy was not in front of Hippo's liquor store.

He had gone with the two Cambridge policemen to stand in the door of the second-floor loft at 1319.

Their arrival had started the Jade Oration.

Silently, Flynn shook hands with the two detectives and handed Randy a peanut butter sandwich and Coca Cola.

Despite the smell, despite the death-encouraging oration, Randy wolfed the sandwich and poured the Coke down his throat with dispatch.

"Why else has Man created these magnificent machines of death, if not to use them? And he will use them and does use them. Consider your poisonous gases outlawed by the Geneva Convention." (Squirt.) "Then consider the poison that pours forth from every smokestack and other waste duct in this world. Is this not forbidden by the Geneva Convention as well? There is a war being waged on this earth—a war of contempt and greed—and these are the weapons of this war. It is a war of the People against themselves!"

Sassie arrived shortly thereafter, in a pleasant beige slack suit, and after wrinkling her nose at the oracle's odor, stood in the doorway with the others and watched and listened.

"Be open in your killing, I say! Rid yourselves of contempt and greed. Murder not by these subtle means, but murder openly, with faith, hope and charity, with kindliness, and with love!"

Flynn said to Sassie, "This is hardly the place for a father of five."

Sassie said, "I trust you see the errors of your ways, Frank."

"I do." Flynn knocked Randy on the head lightly with his knuckles. "I always have."

210

One of the Cambridge detectives said, "We have a circus wagon downstairs, Inspector. We can take care of this monkey."

"What will you do with him?"

Sassie said, "I can take care of it, Frank. This is my bag."

Flynn said to the detectives, "This is Doctor Sarah Fleming."

The detectives shook hands with her.

"I've heard of you," said one.

"Thank you."

"We'd appreciate your help. We've got enough fruitcakes in the cooler now to open a pastry store."

"This one's really gonzo," said the other detective.

"He's very interesting," Sassie said. "He seems perfectly logical, on the basis of his starting axiom."

"Yeah," said the first detective. "He's a real fruitcake."

"Well," Flynn said. "You lads might assume the task of draining the rest of that spray can. It's a simple two-step, you noticed. One step forward, slide, one step back. And I never took a lesson!"

"DROP DEAD!"

Jade, seeing he was losing his audience, raised his volume.

"The LEAST you can do for the world, if you cannot improve it by the simple means of mass murder, is to void the space you presently occupy!"

Flynn said, "Come on, Randy. Let's void the space we presently occupy, and go home to bed."

Sassie said, "Thanks for calling me, Frank. I'll walk our death-champion here through to some kind of therapy."

"Did he blow up the airplane?"

Sassie said, "No. I'm sure not."

"Did you?"

She looked at him in surprise, smiled, and said nothing.

Randy threw his knapsack into the back of the family car—a black Checker—and climbed into the front seat beside his father.

"Good work, lad," Flynn said, as he headed the high, boxy vehicle toward Massachusetts Avenue.

Randy said, "Now do I get to take a shower?"

Flynn sniffed the air.

"I'd recommend it."

Thirty-three

Friday morning, after breakfast, Flynn rinsed his coffee cup and loaded it with Yarrow Flowers tea.

He took it into his study with him, set it on the desk to steep, and closed the door.

It took him only a moment to find the number he wanted in the phone book.

"Wentworth-Methodist. Good morning."

"I haven't got your name," Flynn said.

"Gerry Lasher."

"Are you the minister there?"

"Yes. How can I help you?"

"This is Mister Finnegan, Doctor Lasher," Flynn said. "Of the HSL."

The minister of Wentworth-Methodist Church gasped.

"The Human Survival League," Flynn amended.

"Oh. I see."

"It's our purpose to be helpful," Flynn added.

"Thank God. I thought you might be, you know, that other group—"

"No," said Flynn. "Your congregation is safe from us."

"—I read about in the newspapers."

"I believe you have a family in your congregation by the name of Dickerman?"

"Dickerman. Yes. Dickerman. They used to be members of our congregation."

" 'Used to be'?"

"Yes. I think they moved away. About a year ago."

"They did not move away, Doctor Lasher."

"No? Maybe they joined some other congregation."

"They did not join another congregation, Doctor Lasher."

"Oh. Well, what happened to them? I haven't seen them in about a year, I'd say."

"They fell into serious trouble."

"Oh. I'm sorry to hear that. Anything I can do?"

"Mrs. Dickerman has developed what I would describe as a serious drug problem."

"Oh, that's terrible!"

"Mister Dickerman, not knowing how to handle all this, and probably blaming himself, somewhat, left hearth, home, and family sometime around Christmas."

"Terrible situation. We had one similar to this—"

"You have one now, Doctor Lasher. I believe the Dickerman family needs a certain amount of community support?"

"Yes. Of course."

"In fact, I suspect Mister Dickerman took to the mountains, or wherever, in expectation community support would be more forthcoming and fulsome in his absence."

"We can't do anything about a situation we don't know about."

"Ah, that's where the Human Survival League comes in, Doctor Lasher. We tattle."

"Wasn't there a boy in that family, a son? Little fellow—"

"Yes. Cary Dickerman. He's about fifteen."

"That old?"

214

"That old. But not old enough, by law, to get a job."

"This is one of those situations—"

"It is, indeed," Flynn agreed.

"Is someone at the Dickerman house now?"

"I believe so," answered Flynn. "I saw Mrs. Dickerman last night in an advanced drugged condition. The boy, I suspect, is on his way to school at the moment. A nice lad."

"I'll go over to the house right away. I'll see if Doctor Moore is available. Do you know him?"

"No."

"He's a member of the congregation, and very good in situations of this sort. Very generous with his time. Very understanding. Will the Dickerman woman require hospitalization, do you think?"

"Yes. I think so. Doctor Moore should be able to tell you."

"Well, we'll go over right away. In situations of this sort. . . . By the way," Gerry Lasher asked, "what is the Dickerman woman's first name?"

"I don't know."

"It's much easier, in a situation of this sort, if we know the first name."

"I'm sure it is."

"Thank you very much for calling. By the way, will you and the, uh, Human Surplus, uh, Survival League wish to be involved in this matter any further?"

"No," said Flynn. "We're just bringing this situation to your attention."

"Well, thank you very much. I was just wondering if perhaps you had some funds, which could be used in a situation of this sort—"

"No," said Flynn. "We're not funded."

After hanging up, Flynn had a sip of his tea, and said to himself, "Now to ring Ding-Dong-the-Bell."

"Is this the Headmaster?"

"Yes. This is Jack Lubell."

"Good morning, Mister Lubell. This is Mister Flynn, beaming parent of 'the Flynn Twin,' as you have it."

"Oh, yes. I was talking to Randy yesterday. Did he mention it?"

"Randy's missed school the last day or two."

"Todd, then."

"So has Todd."

"Are they sick?"

"No, I've had them out of school for other reasons."

"We haven't had any luck in finding Randy's violin, Mister Flynn."

"Oh, I'm sorry to hear that."

"I trust you don't mean to make a police action out of this. I mean, as you said—"

"No, that's not why I'm calling, Mister Lubell."

"Oh?"

"Some friends and myself have a little extra money —tax returns, you know—and we've banded together under the banner of the Human Survival League— that's what we're calling ourselves—"

"Cute."

"Isn't it? And we've decided to give one of your students a full scholarship, room, board, and tuition, for as long as it's necessary—"

"Oh, that's wonderful! We have some very interesting candidates. There's this girl from Iran. Her father is having difficulty getting money out of Iran to pay her bills here, such a complicated matter, and—"

"We've picked our recipient."

"Oh?"

216

"Cary Dickerman."

"Cary? Why Cary?"

"Why not Cary?"

"Well, I mean, his family's fully able to pay; they live just down the street. It's almost as if he were boarding here now. Another candidate is this boy from Oklahoma who has applied. From what we've heard, he's a very talented dancer—"

"Cary Dickerman's tuition is in arrears, is it not?"

"Yes, I think so. But that's a temporary matter. He said something about his father's being on an extended business trip, in Pakistan or something—"

"He's a good student?"

"Not lately. His marks have dipped this term. In fact, he may be going on probation. Something seems to be bothering him, you know the way it is with children—"

"I do."

"And then there's a boy named Fox, from the inner city. His father blows glass, at the Boston Center for the Arts—"

"And Cary is on the hockey team?"

"He won't be, if he goes on academic probation."

"Good, then, it's settled," Flynn said. "Cary Dickerman it is."

"Mister Flynn—"

"If you'd do me the favor, Mister Lubell, of never mentioning to young Dickerman that you and I talked. You know, seeing Randy and Todd are his classmates—"

"Of course."

"You might say, when he asks, that his bills are being paid by the Human Survival League, the HSL—"

The Headmaster was silent.

"In the meantime, just enclose his bills with the bills

217

of my own sons, and send them all to me here at the house—"

The Headmaster remained silent.

"And incidentally," continued Flynn, "Cary Dickerman should be moved into the dormitories this afternoon."

"Oh?"

"Yes. Something has come up, suddenly. His mother has to join his father in Pakistan immediately, or something of the sort, and I'm sure Cary doesn't know about it yet. You can find the room for him right away, can't you?"

"It won't be easy, but we will do so."

"That's the spirit!" Flynn said to the Headmaster. "Appreciate all you're doing, Headmaster."

"Yes—" said Jack Lubell.

"Good morning," said Flynn.

Still alone in his den, Flynn drained his teacup, and said to himself, "Now, being the shining fellow he is, I'll bet myself a fistful of parsley Paul Kirkman is at his desk in the Passenger Services Office, sitting up straight in his Zephyr Airways blazer, all ready to have me call him."

Thirty-four

"Ah, Cocky!" Flynn breezed into the office, scaled his hat onto a window seat and dumped his coat on top of it. "I know exactly what my next move is."

At the chessboard, he moved his Bishop to Knight Five.

"Nothing like a good night's sleep. I read about someone having one once."

He sat at his desk.

"What's this? A bulletin from the FBI? And how come all of a sudden I'm on their mailing list?"

"A messenger dropped it off an hour ago," Cocky said. "Marked 'Utmost Secret.' Without an envelope."

"Ah, I see!" Flynn had turned to the last page. "This is why I'm on their mailing list. The sons of bees have stings in their tails. Listen to this, Cocky: 'During this investigation, cooperation from the Boston Police Department, represented by Inspector F. X. Flynn, has not only been minimal, but, at times, obstructive, and, at meetings, Inspector Flynn has been disruptive. . . .' Good! I'm glad they're keeping all that 'utmost secret.' My dear old mother would groan in her grave, if news of that reached her! Where's Grover, by the way?"

"On his way in."

"What does the rest of it say? Ah, yes: the Fibbies list of prime suspects for the blowing up of Flight 80.

Who have they got, now? The Human Surplus League, described here as a 'nationally organized, radical underground group, members and addresses currently unknown; Baird Hastings, theater producer; Mrs. Charles Fleming; Charles Fleming, Junior; Annette Geiger; Alf Walbridge et al.,' whoever they may be. 'Alexander Coffin'? Who's he? 'Passenger,' it says here, from Atlanta, Georgia, 'employed as a bill collector for a public utility company, history of mental problems, known to have self-destructive tendencies, unknown why he was aboard the plane.' One or two others . . . Nathan Baumberg! I knew they'd get him. Hess would put him on any list of suspects he happens to be making up. Now, Cocky, they're doing very well, even without our cooperation, wouldn't you say?

"Hello?" Flynn said into the telephone.

"Da?"

"Todd! Where are you, lad?"

"Cambridge."

"Good lad."

"I called Mom and she said Randy's home asleep and that you and he rounded up the HSL last night."

"We did. We rounded up the whole one hundred and forty pounds of it."

"Was it really just one guy?"

"One guy. With a strong suicidal tendency he has trouble keeping to himself."

"Can I go home now?"

"Of course, lad. Where have you been?"

"Oh, I fell into a sex expansion group."

" 'Sex expansion.' What does that mean?"

"It means what it says, Da."

"I'm not sure what it says."

"People."

"I've got that bit."

220

"They mean to expand one's sexual awareness."

"Yes? And how do they do that?"

"By expanding one's sexual experience, Da."

"Oh? Of fifteen-year-olds?"

"Everybody, Da. One lady there must have been near eighty."

"Bless my left elbow! Was your sexual experience expanded?"

"Yes, sir."

"And did you enjoy it?"

"Yes, sir."

"My right elbow, too! Did you learn anything?"

"Yes, sir."

"And what happened to your pursuit of the HSL?"

"I got distracted, Da."

"It sounds it."

"Da, I'm too pooped to pop."

"I should think so. Would I be guessing right to suspect you need a shot of penicillin?"

"Yes, sir. That would be a good guess."

"Before you go home, stop at the office of Doctor Moore, Ted Moore. I think he's out of his office this morning, but I suggest you go there and wait for him."

"Will you call him?"

"Embarrassed, are you?"

"I might be."

"I'll explain the matter to him. I'll tell him you were infected in the line of duty."

"Thanks, Da."

"Think nothing of it. Are you all right otherwise?"

"Oh, yeah. It was wonderful, Da."

"But all good things come to an end, eh?"

"I'm exhausted."

"Too much of a good thing?"

"I was very popular there."

221

"Delighted to hear it. Say, I forgot to tell Randy I found his violin."

"Where?"

"In a pawnshop. Would you tell him for me, please?"

"Do you know who stole it?"

"Now, how would I know a thing like that?"

"You're a cop."

Flynn said, "I've been distracted. Now hie yourself to Doctor Moore and his needle. I'll explain to your mother."

"Okay."

"The violin is in the back of the police car. I'll bring it home, next time I come. I trust your new sexual sophistication hasn't damaged your ability to play the violin?"

"I don't think so."

"That's good," Flynn said. "See you soon."

As Flynn was looking up the telephone number of the Hotel Royale, Cocky sorted through a pile of notes he had left on the desk.

With his left hand, he picked up one and handed it to Flynn.

"What's this?"

"Insp.—Paul Levitt, sportswriter for the *Herald-American* called. Said he read in his own paper that Percy Leeper, according to witnesses, kept saying 'Peppermint' before he boarded the plane. Paul thought we'd like the solution to this. The next contender for the middleweight crown—the next guy Leeper would fight—is the Puerto Rican boxer, José 'Pepe' Mintz. Funny, uh?"

"It is, indeed," said Flynn. "And did Mister Levitt

222

happen to say if Señor Pepe Mintz wears candy-striped trunks?"

Half of Cocky's face grinned.

Flynn reached for the telephone.

"Now let's put a little pressure on His Excellency, Rashin al Khatid, the Ifadi Minister of the Exchequer."

Cocky's right arm twitched.

"He's alive?"

Flynn said, "I hope so."

"Yes?"

The voice was quiet, almost a whisper. It sounded afraid.

"Excellency?"

There was a hesitation. "Yes?"

"This is Francis Xavier Flynn."

"Good morning, Mister Xavier Flynn. Your guard is still at the door."

"Excellency, from where you are in the suite, can you see Nazim Salem Zoyad and Mihson Taha?"

"No. I am in the bedroom. They are in the living room. The door is closed."

"I wish to talk to you privately. I do not want them listening in."

"It's all right, Mister Xavier Flynn. I have noticed that the telephone extension number in this bedroom is different from the numbers in the living room and the other bedroom."

"Good. Did they hear the phone ring, do you think?"

"I picked it up right away. Also, I hear the television going. Mihson Taha is very fond of these American television programs which give away prizes to the various contestants who—"

"Excellency, I have three or four pieces of information to give you which I think, in your wisdom, should incline you to come clean."

" 'Come clean'?"

"Be honest with me."

"But of course, Mister Xavier Flynn. I—"

"I can't quite put the pieces together myself, but perhaps you can."

"I'm sure I have nothing to say other than what I said to you the other day. My government—"

"—is one of the things I want to talk to you about."

"My government—"

"—is screwing you, Excellency. Will you listen a moment?"

"Of course, Mister Xavier Flynn, but—"

"First, Excellency, your government has canceled the arms deal with the United States."

"Oh? But why should that be? Our mission was entirely successful, the documents are—"

"Second, we have unofficially understood that your government has entered into an arms agreement with the People's Republic of China."

"With Red China? That is highly unlikely, Mister Xavier Flynn. Ideologically, our governments are—"

"Third, your government has issued a statement that you died, of a heart attack, two nights ago, in Ainslee."

"Oh?"

"Were you aware of that?"

"No."

"Sometimes we're the last to know the biggest news concerning ourselves," said Flynn. "You're dead."

"But, obviously, Mister Xavier Flynn—"

"You're taking sustenance."

"—I am alive. My government, in its wisdom—"

"Fourth—the item I think you'll find of most personal significance is that, according to Zephyr Airways

Passenger Services Manager, Paul Kirkman, your seats in Row 17 were not assigned seats."

"Oh?"

"They were reserved seats. Who made your travel arrangements for you?"

"Why, Mihson Taha—"

"And when you boarded Flight 80 to London, who pointed out to you that your seats were in Row 17?"

"Mihson Taha."

"Precisely."

"My head swims—"

"In fact, Excellency, I think the only reason you haven't been murdered already is because I happened to discover you alive and well at the Hotel Royale two days ago. Think about that a moment."

"I don't need to think about that. How soon can you get here, Mister Xavier Flynn?"

"Are you ready?" Flynn said to Grover, who was just coming in.

"Where are we going?"

"Hotel Royale."

"Inspector, I heard on the car radio the FBI has a big break concerning the 707 explosion. We should go to the airport."

"Want to be in for the kill, eh?" Flynn was putting on his overcoat. "We're going to the Hotel Royale."

Cocky handed Flynn another note from the desk.

"What's this, now? More news about Fucker Henry and Pepe Mintz?"

"Insp.—The lab called concerning that human hand you found in your backyard. The report is that the severed hand could not be a result of the aircraft explosion, Tuesday morning. They say that the hand was severed from its body no later than last Saturday noon."

"YE GODS!" said Flynn. "Slapped by my own severed hand!" He screwed on his hat. "Well, there's nothing I can do about that, now. Off we go, Grover. Hotel Royale."

Thirty-five

"Grover, arrest these men!"

Using the key of the policeman guarding the door of the hotel suite, Flynn had stomped into the living room.

Mihson Taha and Nazim Salem Zoyad jumped up from their chairs. They had been sprawled, one on the divan, the other in an armchair, watching, "Win! Win! Win!" on television.

Grover stood inside the open door, looking confused.

"Who?"

"You!"

"Arrest who?"

"These men. Known as Abbott, Carson, or Desmond, Edwards, however you want to book them."

"What for?"

"What for?"

"That's what I said, Inspector! What for?"

"I don't care what for! For watching television in the daytime! For mass murder! It makes no difference to me."

"Inspector, we can't just arrest people."

"Arrest them for carrying a gun without a permit."

"Are they carrying a gun without a permit?"

"If not, give them yours."

"Inspector—"

"Arrest them for obstructing justice."

Mihson Taha and Nazim Salem Zoyad were standing in the room innocently enough, arms at their sides, eyes going back and forth from Grover to Flynn.

"They're not obstructing anything. In fact, we're in their room without a warrant."

The bedroom door opened.

Rashin al Khatid stood in the doorway, impeccably dressed. He folded his arms across his chest.

"Resisting arrest," rolled Flynn.

"They're not!"

"But you are! I never thought I'd live to see the day when you'd resist arresting someone."

"Inspector—"

"Get them out of here!" Flynn pointed to the uniformed policeman. "Put your handcuffs on these men. Lead them downstairs. Put them in a police car. Bring them to headquarters. And book them, damn it! I want to speak to His Excellency here."

Grover said, "Excellency?"

"Now, then, Excellency, you were about to say?"

Rashin al Khatid sat on the edge of the bed, his hands folded neatly in his lap.

Flynn had closed the door to the living room.

"Something further about the wisdom of your government?"

"I don't know what to say, Mister Xavier Flynn."

"I expect you'll find words."

"I believe my life to be in danger, as you said; however I know of no reason why it should be. I have fulfilled my mission. It was not my fault an airplane blew up in the sky. However, when your government announces to the world your death—"

"It leaves one feeling a little uncertain, right?"

"—Yes."

"A little insecure?"

"Yes."

"Even a little curious, perhaps?"

"Mister Xavier Flynn, I have been a little curious from the beginning."

"Oh?"

"Yes. You see, from the beginning I have been asking myself, why me? I am not an important person. I am not a relative of the President or anyone else in the executive branch of our government. Such jobs, especially the job of Minister of the Exchequer, go to very close relatives of the President."

"I daresay."

"I have no family. No family at all. My parents are dead. I have never married. I had a brother, but he was killed in the most recent overturn of the government. At first, I thought it might be because of him, of his death, that I was chosen for this most exalted position. But, no, he was just a simple farmer who was run over at night by a Jeep. A great many people were killed in the most recent overturn of the government, Mister Xavier Flynn. I did not even take part in the overturn myself. I was at home, with a severe cold."

"I'm sorry to hear that."

"Thank you."

"Are you all better now?"

"Oh, it is completely gone, now."

"Good."

"I am just a simple bookkeeper, Mister Flynn. I am not exalted enough to be an accountant, I trust you understand. It is my function in this life to copy down numbers, which my superior gives me, into books. I copy the numbers down in one book in the morning, and another book in the afternoon."

"I've got the idea."

"You can imagine my surprise one morning when my superior came to me and told me to report to the presidential palace. To the President himself. I said, 'But who will copy the numbers into the books?' I still do not know who is copying my numbers into my books, Mister Xavier Flynn."

"So the President made you the Minister of the Exchequer right then?"

"He did me that honor. He showed me my new office in the palace, called for a car, and sent me home to a new house near the palace. Tailors came in the afternoon to make clothes for me. Ever since that magnificent day, I have been a little curious, you see."

"When was this?"

"Just six or seven weeks ago. It has all been very quick. I told myself that I had been chosen for the job because I had never offended the Fates, not to the slightest infraction, never in my life, and that—"

"Did you ever have time to work at the job of Minister of the Exchequer?"

"There seemed very little to do. Mihson Taha, my secretary, is such an efficient man. He always seemed to know what to do and told me the Minister is never to worry. Within a day or two, the President, in lengthy sessions, began explaining to me the nature of this mission. It was all very difficult to understand, but the President was most patient and kind. Then, of course, too, the American businessman, Mister Frings, of the Kassel-Winton Bank, came to visit us on this matter concerning the International Credits, and it was my honor to be his host—"

"And the next thing you knew, you were off on this mission, with your secretary and your bodyguard—"

"It has always been my desire to see the United States of America, or, in fact, to see anywhere."

"—yet you were still curious as to why you had been chosen for this big job."

"I am still curious, Mister Xavier Flynn."

"You speak English well."

"I have been devoted to the learning of English. It is unknown to anyone but my canary, but it is my pleasure in this life to write poetry in English."

"Your canary?"

"I tell you, I am alone in this life. My canary is the only one who has ever heard my poetry in English. I believe it makes her happy. She always sleeps better after hearing my poetry in English. If, in life, one can make even a little bird happy—"

"Thank you."

"A great many people speak English well in my country. My father was a houseman, you see, for—"

"Yes. Do you yet know why you were made Minister of the Exchequer?"

"I am not yet a relative of the President, Mister Xavier Flynn. However, Mihson Taha is."

"Mihson Taha is a relative of the President?"

"Yes. My secretary. He is a third cousin of the President, if I understood correctly. However, he is also a very able man—"

"I'll bet he is."

Flynn opened the door to the living room. Grover, the uniformed policeman, the secretary, and the bodyguard were gone.

"Get your passport," Flynn said to Rashin al Khatid.

"Where are we going, Mister Xavier Flynn?"

"Montreal, Canada. To see a friend. A Chinese friend. A Mister Tsin. But first I need to make a few phone calls."

Thirty-six

"Don't worry." Flynn steered His Excellency, Rashin al Khatid, the Minister of the Exchequer for the Republic of Ifad, by the elbow through the glass doors of Air Canada. "You won't see a Row 17 on this airplane. I'll see to it."

"Even returning to this airport fills me with trepidation, Mister Xavier Flynn. If someone is blowing up airplanes today, I fear I will return to my state of woe. I shall look very carefully for the portents the Fates always leave out for those who wish to be observant."

"See?" Flynn said. "We're boarding through Gate 6. What could be jollier than that?"

The Minister shrugged. "Gate 4."

"Flynn!"

Hess, with two acolytes, was leaving the coffee shop.

"Nice of you to drop by," Hess said. "You must have heard about our break. Who's this?"

"George Harris," Flynn said, quickly calculating his alphabet and coming up with a G-H. "A fishing buddy."

"It is excellent to make your acquaintance, sir." Rashin al Khatid bowed slightly, then extended his hand, which Hess, in amazement at such formality, took. "Although I offend no living creature, be it fowl of the air or fish in the sea, I have heard most seemly things about your fish in the United States of America, in that—"

"Shut up," said Flynn. "He's drunk," Flynn said to Hess. "A bit too much of the airport chowder."

"A drinking buddy, eh, Flynn? You need another one."

"Oh, no, sir—" Rashin al Khatid began, until Flynn stepped in front of him.

"Now, then, Fibby Hess," Flynn said, "what's this big break of yours? Did you finally find a hotel room in Boston?"

The two acolytes smiled at each other over the eccentric Boston policeman.

"The thing may be wrapped up," Hess said.

" 'Thing'?"

"The blowing up of the airplane."

"Oh, that 'thing.' " Flynn nodded sagely. "And what was 'the break' that 'wrapped up' the 'thing'?"

"Fleming."

"Fleming?"

"Fleming."

"Fleming!"

"Charles Fleming, Junior, committed suicide last night. In his rooms. On what-was-it street?" Hess asked an acolyte.

"Forster Street."

"Forster Street. It was in our report that we would interview him today. So we were pretty close."

"Close as a hound's tooth to a rabbit's ass," said Flynn. "Chicky did himself in, did he?"

"You knew him?"

"I'd never seen him."

"Have to step lively, in this game, Flynn."

"And how does Chicky's committing suicide 'wrap up' the murder of over a hundred people?"

"He was pretty heavily in debt. Gambling. We knew that."

"Everybody knew that," said Flynn, "except those of us who had to find out."

"He was in way over his head. His father, the Judge, had always helped him out before. This time he was in debt for more than he could ever pay. I guess his father knew it."

"Yes?" Flynn urged the crowing Hess.

"Well, Flynn, no father takes easily to the idea of his son's knees and elbows being cracked. His spine being broken."

"Entirely understandable," said Flynn. "But you're talking about a Justice of the United States Federal Court. Don't you G-men stick together at all?"

"Exactly. You can't tell me he didn't have a pretty good idea of what would happen to his son if he couldn't pay."

"But a federal judge," said Flynn, "dispensing justice all his life. Murdering over a hundred people?"

"Stranger things have happened. Wouldn't you prefer your son over any hundred other people?"

"I suppose so," said Flynn. "I suppose so."

"Sure, Flynn," Hess said. "It's human nature."

"Here's a man," Flynn said to the acolytes, "with an enviable understanding of his fellow creatures. Simple."

They nodded agreement with Flynn's admiration.

Hess continued, "The Judge took out, or thought he took out, half a million dollars' worth of flight insurance on the trip. Actually, his insurance, by federal law, was restricted to one hundred and twenty-five thousand dollars."

"Always on your toes," said Flynn. "You feds. A law for everything."

"It probably would have been enough to cover Charles Junior's debts."

234

"Until the boxing match," said Flynn.

"What boxing match?" Hess asked.

"Who mentioned a boxing match?" Flynn glared at Rashin al Khatid.

Rashin al Khatid said, "I am not fond of sports of physical violence, although, humbly, I understand you gentlemen might consider them essential to the development of manliness—"

"Hess," Flynn began, "it's an interesting theory, but you need a few connectors, if you see what I mean."

"Theory? Would you buy dying testimony?"

"Sometimes . . . ," Flynn answered. "Have you got any today?"

"Suicide note. In the handwriting of Charles Fleming, Junior. He wrote it while he was dying. He slashed his wrists, and there was blood on the paper."

"And what did the suicide note say?"

Air Canada's flight to Montreal was being announced.

Hess took a step closer to Flynn. "The note said, Mister Flynn, 'He did it for me.' "

"Ach!" said Flynn. " 'He did it for me.' I see. Highly suggestive."

" 'Suggestive'?"

"Well, you see," said Flynn, "the Judge didn't make Chicky the beneficiary of the insurance policies. Does that worry you at all?"

"Of course he wouldn't. He couldn't trust his son. He left it to his widow."

"Are you accusing her, too?"

"No, Flynn," Hess sighed, wearily. "But of course she would pay the son's debts out of her husband's insurance when she found out it was a matter of life and death."

"It's human nature?" asked Flynn.

"Of course."

235

"So you think Charles, Junior, knew his father was going to blow up the plane?"

"No," answered an acolyte. "He figured out what happened later."

"Then what good is this 'dying testimony,' as you call it?"

Again Hess took a step toward Flynn. "Only the Judge and his son knew what they said to each other last Sunday when they took a walk in the woods together. And they're both dead."

"Ah," said Flynn. "That wraps it up, clearly!"

Their flight to Montreal was being announced again.

"Well," Flynn said. "It sounds to me like you've got the basis of a very good report!" He shook hands with Hess. "A very good report, indeed. God bless the FBI and all the little Fibbies!"

"Hurry up." Again Flynn steered His Excellency by the elbow. "We're late for the plane, and I have to make a phone call."

He slammed the door of the phone booth in His Excellency's face.

"Elsbeth?"

"Both boys are home," she said. "Todd came in an hour ago."

"Good, good."

"He called me earlier."

"Good."

"I told him to call you," she said.

"He did."

"Frannie, he seems terribly tired."

"I know."

"Exhausted. To the point of sickness, maybe."

"He's not sick."

"How do you know?"

236

"He's just tired. I'm in a phone booth."

"He was too tired to tell me what he had been doing."

"I'm missing a plane."

"Do you know what he was doing?"

"Yes."

"What was he doing?"

"Oh, Elsbeth. He was in an exercise class."

"Exercise? That's good."

"He said it was nice."

"Two days and two nights he was in an exercise class?"

"Very enthusiastic bunch, he said. Highly motivated class."

"Frannie, he walks funny."

"Just a little stiff."

"Shall I rub him?"

"No. He'll be all right. Just let him sleep. Plenty of eggs and cheese and he'll be all right in no time. I'm missing a plane."

"Where are you going, or shouldn't I ask?"

"I'm going to see Mister Tsin. In Montreal."

"Will you be back tomorrow?"

"I think so. Anything you want in Montreal?"

"You might get some Havana cigars. For the humidor. Guests still like them."

"Okay."

"You remember how to smuggle?"

"Yes: Look innocent and blame my wife. Listen, will you do me a favor?"

"Of course."

"Sassie Fleming."

"You mentioned."

"Will you get to her, at the University, at her house, see if she needs you?"

237

"Of course."

"Tell her, no matter what she hears during the next few hours, the Judge did not blow up that airplane."

"Who says he did?"

"Chicky, the son, committed suicide."

"That's bad enough on her."

"Left an incriminating note, the conceited little skunk."

"That's worse."

"Make her some tea, pour a little sherry, maybe. Make her go ride a horse. That's what she likes."

"All right, Frannie."

"Tell her I'll talk to her when I get back. Goodbye."

Thirty-seven

"You see, I believe His Excellency was never meant to take his seat aboard that airplane," Flynn said. "His secretary, Mihson Taha, who happens to be the cousin of the President of Ifad, purposely made reservations for seats in Row 17 of that airplane, knowing His Excellency would never sit in Row 17, and then, once aboard, pointed out the Row number to His Excellency, causing His Excellency to leave the airplane."

"I see that."

Mister Tsin lay on the couch, bouncing his basketball on his flat stomach.

"The question is why. And you think the answer is in the People's Republic of China?"

"I do," said Flynn.

Rashin al Khatid sat on a straight chair in the library of the hilltop gray stone mansion like a student at a conference between his parents and his teacher, wondering what disposition would be made of "his problems."

Flynn said, "I believe our innocent bookkeeper from Ifad has been set up for something, put up as a decoy to set up somebody else. But I don't know who else was being set up, or why."

"Ummmm," said Tsin.

Flynn and Rashin al Khatid had arrived in Montreal

239

shortly before four o'clock Friday afternoon, and taxied through the clean, snowy streets to a hilltop overlooking the city.

The mansion had an extraordinary arrangement of what appeared to be television antennae on its mansard roof.

Flynn knew them to be a complete combination of radio transmitters, receivers, and silent monitors. He was aware of Mister Tsin's function in the Canadian city just north of the United States border.

They were shown into the library by a compatriot houseman, given tea, and told Mister Tsin was being summoned presently.

Mister Tsin appeared before they finished their tea.

A lean man in his forties, Tsin wore a sweatsuit with the emblem of an American university on its chest.

"Forgive me," he said, "for not being here when you arrived. I was in the barn, practicing basketball. I wasn't sure precisely when you would arrive, and I so love the game."

There was sweat on his forehead and snow on the toes of his sneakers.

"How do you do, Comrade Minister?" Bracketing his basketball under one elbow, Tsin extended his hand to Rashin al Khatid. "I was so sorry to hear of your untimely demise of a heart attack. Such a young man. Are you feeling better now that Mister Flynn has resuscitated you?"

"I am enjoying good health, thank you," began Rashin al Khatid. "I have always observed the strictest dietary laws, you see, and remained moderate in—"

"And you, Mister Flynn? I am so glad to see that so many reports I have heard that you, too, are dead, are false."

"Is that what you've heard?" brazenly inquired Flynn.

"Actually, I had heard you had survived as a vegetable, hospitalized in New Zealand. Or was it Switzerland? Perhaps it was Sweden?"

"I am perfectly well," said Flynn.

"Two dead men in my own house," Tsin said, bouncing the basketball on the hardwood floor. "Perhaps someone in your religious traditions has been so honored, but I doubt such a curious honor has befallen a representative of the People's Republic of China, to this point."

"Oh, no," said Rashin al Khatid. "Let me assure you that in the writings of——"

"Basketball," Tsin said, firmly, "is an old Chinese game."

"Is it, indeed?" said Flynn.

"The ancestors of basketball," Tsin asserted in rhythm with the bouncing ball, "are Chinese."

Then Tsin threw himself onto the couch.

Playing with the ball, he listened to Flynn.

He said "Ummmm," occasionally.

The only time he looked at Flynn was when Flynn mentioned the unofficial report that the People's Republic of China had agreed to sell half a billion dollars' worth of arms to the Republic of Ifad.

Looking away again, he repeated "Ummmm."

"My guess," Flynn concluded, "is that the bomb aboard Flight 80 was planted by Mihson Taha and Nazim Salem Zoyad."

The Minister of the Exchequer sucked in his breath. He looked aghast.

"A very good guess," Tsin said to his basketball. "I should think."

"Well," Flynn said. "You're the translator."

Tsin swung himself into a sitting position, the basketball beside him on the couch.

"And I shall translate," said Tsin, "at breakfast tomorrow morning. After I communicate with Peking. Which is why you came here. Correct?"

"Righty-o," said Flynn.

"Unfortunately," Tsin said, standing up, "I am obliged to fly to Quebec City, for a dinner. Unfortunately, I am embarrassed by not being able to ask my houseguests to accompany me, as you are not expected."

Flynn smiled at this unlikely courtesy.

"The best favor you can do me," he said, "is an early kip and an early bed."

"Of course, Mister Flynn. That will be arranged. Is there anything else we can do for you?"

"Cigars," Flynn said. "Havana cigars, for my wife."

"Ah, yes," said Tsin. "Very illegal to get in the United States. I will have a supply for you at breakfasttime. It is wondrous, is it not? How major conflicts of ideology can be reduced to so much smoke?"

Flynn said nothing.

Taking his basketball with him, Tsin went to the library door, and turned around.

"It is also remarkable, Mister Flynn, how much— as we concern ourselves with the problems of emerging nations and the Third World—we find ourselves dealing more and more with your organization—No Name."

"The world is getting smaller," said N. N. 13. "Isn't it just?"

Thirty-eight

"I regret to inform you gentlemen," Tsin said, as he buttered his toast, "that this morning a ship from the People's Republic of China carrying arms to the Republic of Ifad sank, without a trace, in the Persian Gulf.

"Very surprising," he continued, biting into his toast, "seeing it was such a big ship."

With the eyes of both Francis Xavier Flynn and Rashin al Khatid on him, Tsin applied his fork to his plate. First, he tasted the scrambled eggs mixed with Canadian bacon; then he tasted the home-fried potatoes and fried tomato slices.

Rashin al Khatid was not enjoying Tsin's breakfast.

"Although a ship flying the colors of the People's Republic of China, and fully crewed by our comrade sailors, thankfully enough possession of the ship had been assumed, by standard prearrangement, by five agents of the Republic of Ifad, in Singapore."

Tsin tasted his sausage.

"Therefore, as the ship was in the possession of the Republic of Ifad, I fear your nation, Comrade Minister, has suffered a terrible loss."

"The ship sank?" His Excellency asked.

"Airplanes explode," Tsin shrugged. "Ships sink."

"Has China been paid for those arms?" asked Flynn.

"That's the dicey part," said Tsin. "From what we've

243

been able to discover—thanks to your help, Mister Flynn—China was not going to be fully paid. Note that I said 'fully paid.' "

"I so note," noted Flynn.

Tsin was wearing a different sweatsuit at breakfast, with the emblem of a different American university on its chest.

His basketball was beside his chair.

"My understanding at the moment, from what you've told me, Mister Flynn, and from whatever else I've been able to find out, is that our friend here, His Excellency, The Bookkeeper, absolutely without friends or relatives, but with a good command of English, was raised from obscurity to the post of Minister of the Exchequer of the Republic of Ifad, to perform one simple duty: to die twice, and be murdered once."

Rashin al Khatid was not touching his own breakfast.

"He was sent on this mission to the United States. As he understood it, his mission was to convert a quarter of a billion dollars' worth of his nation's gold into a quarter of a billion dollars' worth of International Credits, which then would be spent purchasing a quarter of a billion dollars' worth of arms from the United States. Very simple. It almost could have been accomplished by phone. Your mission, Excellency"— Tsin chewed in Rashin al Khatid's direction— "was almost totally unnecessary.

"Then why were you sent on it?" Tsin asked rhetorically.

"To provide your government, Comrade Excellency, the necessary time—just a few days, really—to swindle the People's Republic of China."

Rashin al Khatid's white dress shirt didn't look too bad, considering he had been obliged to wear it five days in a row. It was still reasonably white and smooth.

Flynn wondered if His Excellency had been washing it himself in the privacy of his bath.

"At the same time your government, Excellency, had been negotiating with the United States for the purchase of a quarter of a billion dollars' worth of arms, it was negotiating with the People's Republic of China for the purchase of a half a billion dollars' worth of arms.

"Unfortunately, Your Excellency, your nation only had a quarter of a billion dollars worth of gold."

His Excellency's face was becoming as gray-white as his shirt.

"How could the People's Republic of China be so gulled? We were selling Ifad a half a billion dollars' worth of arms for a quarter of a billion dollars' worth of gold, and a quarter of a billion dollars' worth of International Credits. Our representatives looked and saw the gold. In the hours after the explosion of Flight 80, our representatives looked and saw Ifad also had a quarter of a billion dollars' worth of outstanding International Credits.

"This credit balance remained outstanding, wrongly, for days.

"Why? Because the United States government, in its duplicity, did not do the right thing. Only they knew you, and your documents, were aboard Flight 80. Perhaps they presumed Ifad's failure to turn over the quarter of a billion dollars' worth of gold was because Ifad was not only mourning your loss, but also had not received your set of documents. The United States did not make your supposed presence aboard Flight 80 internationally known, because you had been traveling on phony United States passports, and the United States did not wish to have the fact that it was issuing phony passports to Arabian arms buyers internationally known.

"Therefore, there was, what is called, a diplomatic pause."

Tsin pushed his empty plate away from him with his thumb.

"Ifad's gold was on its way to China. Chinese arms were on their way to Ifad. The American arms deal was canceled, to cause the United States to be even slower in questioning Ifad's line of International Credits.

"And your second death, of a heart attack at your desk in Ainslee, was announced by your government.

"And all this time, you were sitting, quite innocently enough, in a hotel room in Boston, with your documents, just in case you and your documents had to be rushed forward to quell any last-minute suspicions of my government in Peking.

"Once the Chinese arms reached Ifad, Comrade Excellency, you would have suffered a third death—one a bit more real to you. You would have been murdered."

Rashin al Khatid was pale.

It took him a moment to work his throat.

"Why would my government do such a devious thing?"

"Your government, Your Excellency," Flynn said, "is hardly interested in the business of governing at all."

"As is so often the case," said Tsin.

"More," continued Flynn, "it's interested in being in the arms business."

Tsin said, "In being an arms supplier to other nations."

"I would have been murdered?" Rashin al Khatid's throat was raspy. "By my government? By Mihson Taha and Nazim Salem Zoyad?"

Tsin shrugged. "A man can die only so many times, Comrade Excellency."

246

Slowly, with pauses caused by weakness, Rashin al Khatid turned from the table and stood up.

He bowed slightly.

He said, "Excuse me."

Slowly, a man dazed, he left the dining room, closing the door softly behind him.

Tsin, leaning forward, arms folded on the table, had watched him go.

"Got to slap these Goddamned, Third World nations around, Flynn," he said. "Until they learn some manners."

Flynn took out his pipe and tobacco pouch.

"This wasn't really an emerging nation or Third World problem," said Flynn. "More a matter of cutthroats and thieves. Pirates, really."

Tsin chuckled. "It's quite marvelous, really. The little bastards actually tried to con the United States of America and the People's Republic of China. We forget that they still think they can."

Flynn lit his pipe, without a word.

Shaking out his match, he asked, "And what will happen to our excellent bookkeeper friend?"

"We'll find room for him somewhere," answered Tsin. "We can always use another astute observer of the Middle East."

"I doubt you'll have one in him."

"Nothing teaches like experience, Flynn. Rashin al Khatid is now an experienced man."

"He is that."

"More tea, Flynn?"

"I'd better wend my way. Something called a Grover is meeting my plane in Boston."

Before leaving the dining room, Tsin took a box from a buffet and handed it to Flynn.

"Cigars," he said. "For your wife."

"Very kind of you," said Flynn, "I'm sure. Tell me, Tsin, where is the Ifadi gold?"

Tsin shrugged. "Ships that pass in the night. Some sink. Some don't."

"The gold is in China?"

"It will plug the teeth of thousands and thousands of Chinese workers. Think of that, Flynn."

"I'll bet."

Tsin opened the front door.

Flynn lit his pipe again. "And did the Chinese ship carrying arms really sink?"

"No. The five Ifadi agents were thrown overboard," Tsin said. "They sank."

Thirty-nine

"Sorry to have to ask you to stop by on a Saturday, Frank." Boston Police Commissioner Edward D' Esopo stood up, coatless and tie askew, behind his desk and held out his ham-like hand. "I know you want to get home."

Again, Captain Reagan was sitting in a side chair in full parade dress, appropriate for either a wedding breakfast or a funeral supper.

"Happened to be passing by anyway," Flynn said, shaking hands with the Commissioner.

Flynn sat in a curved-back leather chair near the desk. He slid the desk ashtray toward him.

The Commissioner sat down and put his hands behind his head.

"I suppose you know why we wanted to see you, Frank."

"Rotation?"

Flynn knocked his pipe bowl against the ashtray.

"What's rotation?" the Commissioner asked Captain Reagan.

Captain Reagan laughed and waved his hand as if swatting flies.

"It's Inspector Flynn's word for sending Captain Walsh's nephew back to the beat."

"I don't want to talk about that now." The Com-

249

missioner swung himself in his swivel chair to face the desk. He put his forearms flat on the desk and folded his hands. "Truth is, Frank, no one can win 'em all."

"I've heard," said Flynn.

"And no one," added the Commissioner, "can deal with the feds. Not for long, anyway."

"The Fibbies want me off the case, is that it?"

"What are 'Fibbies'?" the Commissioner asked the Captain.

Reagan said, "Those who fib?"

"The FBI," drawled Flynn.

"That's it, Frank. They say you're never around. That you've been no help to them. They don't understand half of what you say—and I think they may have a point, there. You went out and arrested the widow of a federal Judge—"

"—only for lunch."

"They don't accept your solution to the Human Surplus League."

With a penknife, Flynn was scraping the inside wall of the bowl of his pipe into the ashtray.

"And I agree with what you said at first, Frank," the Commissioner continued. "This really isn't a matter for the Boston Police. You called this assignment 'baby-sitting.' I really don't blame you for not wanting to sink your teeth into it."

"Thank you."

Flynn blew air through his pipe.

"You needed some time off."

"Thank you."

"I'm glad you took it."

"Indeed, indeed."

"What's really needed here, in this liaison position, is more of a diplomat."

"Indeed."

"More their idea of a cop."

"Ah, yes." Flynn peered down the stem of his pipe. "May I offer a candidate?"

"Ah," Reagan sighed. "Up comes the name of Sergeant Whelan again."

"I've already assigned Captain Reagan, Frank."

Reagan slapped his thigh and laughed. "I'll be retired a hundred years before this one is solved!"

"Oh, I don't know. The FBI say they're very close to a solution now," the Commissioner said.

"Charles Fleming, Junior, and his Da?" asked Flynn.

"Why, no." The Commissioner looked at a piece of paper on his desk. "Hastings. Baird Hastings. The theater producer."

"Good, good," said Flynn. "That's a solution that won't embarrass the People's Republic of China, The Republic of Ifad, or the United States of America. It won't even embarrass Baird Hastings."

The Commissioner's great bull eyes blinked at him.

"Anyway," Flynn added, "I know they won't find a solution in 'Alf Walbridge et al.' "

"Who's that?" asked the Commissioner.

"Fucker Henry's manager. You know, if there really were an FBI all these years, there couldn't possibly be an 'et al.' "

"Frank, what are you saying?"

"Just mumbling," said Flynn. "It's the shock of being dismissed."

"Well." The Commissioner ran his eyes over his desk. He grabbed another piece of paper. "Here's a case that might interest you, Frank."

"Oh?" Flynn put his dead pipe in his mouth.

"Yeah. Two men were released from jail this morning, on a writ of habeas corpus, and were gunned down on the sidewalk, before they could hail a taxi. Machine-

251

gunned." The Commissioner looked at the Captain. "Sounds like an old-time gangland slaying, doesn't it?"

"What were they in for?" asked Flynn.

The Commissioner consulted his paper. " 'Conspiracy to Commit a Misdemeanor'—whatever the hell that means."

"What were their names?" asked Flynn.

"Ah—Abbott and Carson. And they had United States passports to prove it. Gave their addresses as the Hotel Royale." The Commissioner laughed. "Pretty expensive place to conspire to commit a misdemeanor!"

"I wonder—" said Flynn.

The Commissioner looked at him. "What?"

"Well, I'm thinking." Flynn left the dead pipe in his mouth a moment, and then removed it. "Captain Walsh's nephew—as he's known in this office—has been working with me sometime now. And I'm just wondering if this wouldn't be a good case for him to take charge of by himself. His first case, on his own. You know, let him have it."

Reagan groaned. "Sergeant Whelan again."

"Grover," Flynn growled.

"Not a bad idea, Frank," said the Commissioner.

"You know, give the kid a break, and all. Seeing you tell me he did so well at the Police Academy, don't you know?"

"Is he up to it, Frank?" the Commissioner asked.

Flynn answered, "He is, if anybody is."

"Well, good idea, Frank. Captain Reagan will see where the case is at the moment and perhaps get in touch with your Sergeant Grover."

"Whelan," said Reagan.

"Whelan," said the Commissioner.

"Lovely," said Flynn. "Lovely."

Hands flat on the desk, the Commissioner raised himself to a standing position.

"Well, my desk is reasonably clear for a Saturday afternoon." He beamed at Flynn. "Not even a shoe box on it."

"My 'lunch,' " chuckled Flynn.

"Whose hand was that, anyway, Frank?"

"I have no idea," said Flynn. "No idea at all."

Forty

"I'm sure you're right, Grover. I'm sure you're right. Good night."

Flynn slammed the door of the black Ford.

He had had quite enough of Grover's complaints on the ride home that Flynn had so mishandled their involvement in the biggest criminal case in the history of Boston that now Grover would never be able to work for the Federal Bureau of Investigation. Even Flynn's having put Grover in for a case of his own did not soften Grover's anger and disappointment.

The Ford accelerated harshly, and screeched around the corner to the left.

"You'd think somebody wanted him home," Flynn said to himself.

Violin under his arm, Flynn went through the gate, along the walk toward the large, Victorian house.

A jet airplane taking off from Boston's Logan Airport thundered across the harbor.

Flynn looked up at it, as it came over the house. A great monster. A 747, window lights along its length, even in its great, obscenely sagging belly. Its red and green lights winked in a frantic, threatening rhythm. The noise of its huge engines was horrible.

Flynn felt like reaching up and grabbing it down from the sky.

Instead, the jet roaring away in the sky, he climbed the steps to the porch of his house and, with his free hand, worked his key in the lock.

"Oh, God," Flynn said. "I want my tea."

ALSO BY GREGORY MCDONALD

Fletch's ~~trip to Brazil wasn't exactly planned, but it's~~ Carnival time in ~~Rio de Janeiro, and there's justice, thanks~~ to a little arrangement made stateside. ~~And he's got time~~ to hook up with the luscious Laura Soares. Fletch is beginning to relax, just a little. But somehow, he ends up connected to a thirty-year-old unsolved murder, a more recent suicide, and an inconvenient heart attack, and one of these connections might just shorten his own life.

Crime Fiction/0-375-71347-6

FLETCH, TOO

After a few delays, it looks like Fletch is finally getting hitched. A letter arrives from Africa, signed by Fletch's supposedly dead father, inviting the couple to Nairobi for the honeymoon. As soon as they land in Africa, the search for Fletch Sr. begins. There's a murder at the airport, reports of the old man's incarceration, and the evasive hospitality of pop's best friend, who flies them across the continent, just a step or two behind (or maybe ahead of) the old rascal.

Crime Fiction/0-375-71353-0

ALSO AVAILABLE

Confess, Fletch, 0-375-71348-4
Fletch, 0-375-71354-9
Fletch and the Widow Bradley, 0-375-71351-4
Fletch Won, 0-375-71352-2
Fletch's Fortune, 0-375-71355-7

VINTAGE CRIME/BLACK LIZARD
Available at your local bookstore, or call toll-free to order:
1-800-793-2665 (credit cards only).